· THE ·
VARIETY
ARTISTES

· THE ·
VARIETY
ARTISTES
Tom Wakefield

SERPENT'S
TAIL

BRITISH LIBRARY CATALOGUING IN PUBLICATION DATA

Wakefield, Tom
The variety artistes
I. Title
823′.914[F]
ISBN 1-85242-138-X

First published 1987 by Robert Hale Ltd
Copyright © 1987 by Tom Wakefield

This edition first published 1988 by
Serpent's Tail, Unit 4, Blackstock Mews, London N4
Printed on acid-free paper by
Nørhaven A/S, Viborg, Denmark

For
Robert Clayton, Robert Collie and
U. A. Fanthorpe

'She was highly gifted in the art of human intercourse which consists in delicate shades of self-forgetfulness and in the suggestion of universal comprehension.'

Nostromo, Joseph Conrad

1

The Orinocco is said by some to be a tributary of the Amazon. The Amazon is the world's longest river, almost traversing a continent. This should not compel us to dismiss the Orinocco out of hand. It is in its own right a formidable mass of water.

Like a contented seal, Lydia Poulton flopped onto her left side as she lay in the bath and viewed the large varicose veins which bulged clear and blue down the back of her right thigh. The nicknames she had thought up herself. It was the only way she could come to terms with the horrible things. She had at last come to accept them. She fingered the smaller vein gently. 'Orinocco.' Such a romantic sound, so nice to say it aloud, 'Orinocco'.

She had tried to rid herself of them long before Henry had died. Perhaps unfairly, she had lain the blame on the veins. It was Henry who had suggested the single beds. He had said he was sleeping badly and that it was about time they struck out and went a bit modern. He had re-papered the bedroom – all tiny flowers – and he had their large bed removed. It was given to the Social Services. His single bed was one side of the room and hers the other. To complete it all, he bought duvets.

'No more bother with blankets, old girl,' he had said.

The duvet was warm; it crept all about her. Strange how it never slipped off. In the double bed she had warmed her feet on Henry. Her feet got cold quickly and it was necessary for Lydia to buy a hot-water bottle. For after the floral wallpaper, the single beds, the duvets . . . Henry never touched her again.

'Goodnight, old girl,' he would say and then put off the light. After twenty-five years she felt she had switched him off. Just like the light.

The veins were too heavy for an operation. In any event Lydia feared hospitals. However, she had undergone some fearful and painful injections in the hope of making the veins disappear. Huge injections they were. More sensible for a horse than a woman. They had made her legs ache but the veins had remained. She had worn a special bandage and lain diligently with her legs raised over her head. Henry's indifference to her attempts at making herself attractive to him and herself finally forced her to cherish the veins rather than hate them. It would not matter what she looked like, for her husband had withdrawn from his role as a lover. It was a shock that she had not expected. She had always been used to having that side of the marriage. Not as excessively as in their younger days, as it was nearly every night then. After the children had left home it had dwindled to once or twice a week and then Henry stopped it. Not gradually, but suddenly. He carried on as though nothing different had happened to their marriage and would discuss his forthcoming retirement with her.

'Five more years and I finish. We'll sell up this place and get a bungalow in Bournemouth. You've always liked Bournemouth. I'll be sixty-one then, old girl, and you'll be chasing me. There's only a year between us.'

She hadn't answered him. Bournemouth was the same as anywhere else. Lydia became morose. Henry told their children that she was going through the change of life and not to take too much notice of her moods. Lydia had not become moody, but lonely. Therefore she was not as talkative as she had formerly been and could not show the previous sense of wonder she had had in the size of Henry's home-grown tomatoes or the projected new life in Bournemouth.

Three weeks after his retirement, he suffered a stroke and died. For Lydia it was like losing a sister she had not seen for years. She cried a bit at the funeral. What else was there to do? He had left her reasonably provided for. She had a house and his pension. She did not feel bereft, but free. Her son Derek and her daughter Barbara failed to recognize this and dutifully sought to fulfil their obligations to their mother in the way they imagined would be pleasing to her.

Lydia clambered out of the bath. She adjusted her plastic headcap. Steam affected her soft perm badly. She opened the bathroom window just an inch or so to let the steam out of the room. Her son was to have fixed an extractor fan but had forgotten about it. Lydia did not choose to remind him as she disliked having things done for her. Derek always did it in such a busy way that it made her feel inadequate, helpless – yes, even old. Besides, as she clutched the two bathtowels about her large and fleshy body, she enjoyed the whirling vapours that drifted in half-rings about the room. She patted herself dry and looked into the mirror and consoled herself. Her eyes were a pretty blue, and her teeth were all her own.

'It's an outsize, Mother, but the colour is sensible, and it will give you plenty of room,' her daughter had said when she gave Lydia the brown towelling dressing-robe the previous Christmas. She had asked Lydia to put it on show immediately. Being of a docile nature, Lydia had quickly obliged.

'Oh, it suits you. It's really cosy and comfortable looking,' Barbara had said.

Lydia had expressed thanks and enthused.

She took the robe from where it hung behind the bathroom door and hauled herself into it. Brown, why brown? Lydia would have preferred pink. And why so large? There was room enough to get another woman inside it twice her size. True, a smaller one might have been a bit tight about the breasts. Lydia's breasts hung like great handbells. She resented the idea of hiding them in layers of towelling. Large breasts on a young woman had never been out of fashion as regards the tastes of some men.

When the children were younger, the roof of the house had developed a leak and Lydia had heard the two builders discussing that part of her anatomy as they sat astride the roof. She stood beneath the attic hole afraid to move lest they caught her listening.

'Nice tits, Alf. Nice big pair of tits.'

'Yeah, I'd like to get my head between that pair,' the other one had answered.

She ought to have been shocked, but she wasn't. She wasn't used to receiving that kind of compliment and, in spite of the rather uncouth nature of expression, a tremor of excitement had seized her. Henry had made love to her that night. She had instigated the proceedings. At one stage she had got quite carried away and cried, 'Eat me, Henry, eat me!'

'Are you going funny?' he had said and was quite put off.

Even that time Lydia had curbed her demonstrations of passion and lacerated all verbal responses. It did seem a bit silly though just to pant and breathe. It often ruined the timing of things so that Henry suddenly grunted and seconds after was asleep. This left her alert, awake, unsatisfied and strangely apart. Even this was better than the final nothing which eventually happened so suddenly.

Lydia thought of the builders on the roof, removed her plastic hat and fluffed her hair with her fingers. They must be quite old now. I wonder if they still appreciate big tits . . . She put the kettle on to boil and lit the gas. She enjoyed a morning cup of tea alone. It was Saturday, another weekend to get through. Lydia sighed.

'It's our turn this week, Mother.' Her son had telephoned her. (He was very reliable, like his father.) 'Barbara had you over last week, didn't she?'

'Yes, dear.'

'I'll collect you in the car, about 10 a.m. I'll bring the children with me. It will take them off Eileen's hands for a bit. OK?'

'Yes, dear,' Lydia had confirmed the appointment. Her children made her feel like a tennis ball. Over to one in Surrey one weekend, over to the other in Hertfordshire the next. She preferred London but acquiesced in this routine. She did not wish to hurt their feelings. She had always been a quiet, understanding but misunderstood mother.

'Everything all right then, Mother?' Lydia gulped her tea. Her son's question was a formality and did not require an answer. He gave her no time for an answer. He did not sit down and join her at the kitchen table but hovered about her. He was an under-manager at a bank. The sedentary nature of his work seemed to affect him during his leisure time in that he never appeared still.

'I don't want to hang about. The children are waiting for

us in the car. No point in bringing them in. I promised Eileen I'd call in for some roller-blinds for our lounge. We ordered them in the week. They make them to your specific window proportions. Curtains are out now.'

'What next?' Lydia was thinking of duvets.

'Pardon, Mother?' he asked.

'I was wondering what would happen to the curtains. It seems a pity to . . .'

'We are putting them in the children's rooms.'

'Oh, good,' Lydia stood and lifted her weekend case. She balanced her raincoat over her arm. Her son smiled at her as though she were a customer at the bank asking for a loan.

'Ready, then?'

'Yes, dear.' She followed him to the car.

The children began quarrelling before she had climbed into the vehicle. She winced at their grumblings. Both boys wanted to sit in the front seat next to their father. Lydia was about to usurp the position. If she sat in the front, the matter would be settled simply. Also Lydia really felt the need of the extra leg-room the seat offered. She placed her raincoat over the back of the seat. Both boys glared at her, hostile, unsympathetic.

'Hello, dears,' she murmured brightly.

'It's my turn for the front seat, Granny.' The older boy's boldness bit into her.

'Trevor was in the front on the way here. It's my turn to sit in the front going back.'

Lydia stood her ground and left her coat on the seat.

'Mother, would you mind?' Her son had already lifted up her coat. The older boy had vacated his place in the back and Lydia squeezed herself in beside the smaller child. Her knees were pushed upwards and she felt her suspender dig into her thigh.

'I've bought you one of those little trucks, Desmond. It's in my bag. We can look at it when we get home.' Lydia addressed the younger boy and slid her arm around his shoulder as she spoke. He drew away from her.

'I wanted to sit in the front.' The older boy laughed at his brother's displeasure.

'No more nonsense from you two.' Her son started

the engine of the car. Lydia gave each boy a peardrop and smiled through her present state of inward hurt and physical indignity. It was not in her nature to sulk.

'How do I look, Mummy?' Lydia's daughter-in-law came into the comfortable and heavily carpeted lounge where Lydia was perched on an armchair. The two children sat on the settee with eyes glued to the television set. Some game was in progress whereby adult married couples chanced the opportunity of winning washing-machines, refrigerators, electric hair-dryers and any number of such necessary objects for marital bliss by getting ping-pong balls into a goldfish bowl as quickly as possible. Lydia's thoughts wandered from the screen although her eyes were fixed in its direction. She looked at Eileen and appraised the brightly flowered evening dress which adorned her.

'It looks very nice, dear. You'll be the belle of the ball.'

Eileen frowned and gave Lydia a sorrowful, condescending smile. 'It's not a ball, Mummy. Derek's told you, dear, it's a dinner and dance. Organized by the different branches of the bank for employees. All the top people will be there. Things have changed, dear. Social contacts are most important if Derek is to get on. Derek could be a manager in three years if all the cards fall right, and we all have to do our best to support him.' Lydia for the life of her could not comprehend how Eileen, dolled up like a dog's dinner, going to eat, drink and dance, constituted making any sacrifice for her husband. She made it sound like a duty.

'We should be back by 1 a.m. Let the children have a cup of Ovaltine or chocolate at eight, no more than three chocolate biscuits each, and see that they are in bed for half-past eight. If you decide to go to bed before we get back, you won't forget to turn off the television, will you, dear? And don't forget to pull the plug out, and whatever you do, don't bolt the door or we won't be able to get in, dear. Now, are you sure you're comfortable?'

Eileen addressed her mother-in-law in the practised way she related to her children. Organized, formal – with a posture of concern and affection which Lydia found both hurtful and humiliating. Lydia masked her feelings and smiled and nodded. Strange how Eileen could make a Saturday evening's baby-sitting stint seem like a favour. Try as she would, Lydia was not over-fond of her grandchildren. They were averse to a cuddle and on the occasions when she had attempted such demonstrations of affection she had gently but firmly been chided by Eileen.

'They are growing boys, Mother, and I know you wouldn't want them to turn into anything soppy when they are older.'

This rather caring but cold routine and ritual which both parents had agreed on tended to place their grandmother in the role of an elderly child who had to be tolerated because it was their duty to do so. Any help which Lydia offered about the house when she stayed with them was accepted in the light that it was good for the old lady to be occupied. She did not feel old, but her children and grandchildren seemed intent on making her as ancient as possible.

Lydia did not express her resentment but merely added, 'That scent is lovely, dear, really gentle but quite distinct. What is it called?'

'It's not scent, Mumsy. Just a light skin perfume. It isn't the sort of occasion where one would wear scent. Derek doesn't like heavy perfume and I must say I find the heavy stuff that some women wear most cheapening.' Lydia felt herself blushing under her face-powder and rouge. She had always doused herself generously with Lily of the Valley since she was eighteen. She adored its pungent fragrance and had even dabbed some on at her husband's funeral. She pretended not to comprehend Eileen's clever disapproval.

'Well, have a lovely time, dear, and don't worry, I'll look after things this end. I won't forget anything. Enjoy yourself. You're only young once, dear.'

'Mumsy, I'm thirty-two, married with two children.'

Lydia was constantly reminded of Eileen's status in this way. Before she could think of anything consoling to say to her, Derek entered.

'Everything all right?' He spoke brusquely and smiled brightly as though he were checking up on a counter clerk.

'Yes, thank you, dear. See that both of you have a nice time.'

Lydia was pleased to hear the door close behind them, and the noise of the car leaving the garage prompted her to kick off her shoes and settle more comfortably into the chair. She tried to chat to her grandchildren. She had recently visited the Tower of London and thought they might be interested in some of the dramas which had encompassed that historic fortress.

'Oh, shush, Gran, shush. You're spoiling the programme. We were trying to watch.'

Lydia felt obsolete and took refuge in a book she had hidden under the seat of her chair. Its substance was a romantic and sensuous account of the trials and tribulations of a black slave girl who was in the process of triumphing over lost love, rape and fearful ill-treatment in a Southern US cotton plantation. Although it was only fiction, Lydia identified with the heroine throughout all the mishaps which frequented every other page. She was astonished at the girl's powers of survival and quietly envied some of the sensual and passionate aspects of her harsh but none the less eventful existence.

A gun-shot exploded through the lounge. This made Lydia jump and deflected her attention from the rampant plantation overseer who was seeking to force his attentions on the brave heroine amongst the bales of cotton. She closed the book sharply and pushed it under the cushion cover. She was relieved to see a cowboy clutching a gun on the television screen.

'Is it a Western?'

'Shush, quiet, Gran. He's an escaped cavalry man. Clint Eastwood.'

'Oh, I like him.'

'Quiet, Gran, we're trying to watch.' The older boy stamped his foot on the carpet. Lydia ignored his irritation.

'It's nine o'clock. I'll make your cocoa for you or your mum and dad will shoot me when they get back if they know you were not in bed at the right time.'

She prepared the tray containing the drinks and the parental prescription of biscuits and returned. Clint

Eastwood was not on top of a horse. He lay astride a naked young woman, who seemed to be as pleased with the situation as he was.

'Oh, dear, I'm not sure you ought to be watching this, my loves.'

'It's an "X", Gran. Can we watch it? Mum never lets us watch "X"s.'

'Doesn't she, dear?' Lydia took a small bottle from her handbag and dabbed on a sprinkling of Lily of the Valley behind her ear. 'Cheap', that's what Eileen had said about it. Lydia felt wilful.

'Can we watch it? We'll be quiet and won't twit on you.' The older boy patted her hair and looked imploringly into her eyes. This unusual display of affection decided the matter. If she sat and watched the film with the children, she could always cover their eyes when things got hotted up. Most of the women in the film (and there were at least eight) seemed to feel much the same way about Clint Eastwood as Lydia did. She sipped her cocoa and was soon mesmerized as the plot unfolded.

At one stage, when the anti-hero was forced to have his leg amputated, it all looked rather gory. Lydia shuddered. She felt that the children shouldn't be looking. She turned towards them and was relieved to see that both boys had fallen asleep. Contented, she sat and absorbed the rest of the film, feeling more relaxed in spite of the sad ending.

'You'd better not have a second glass of wine, Mother,' said Derek, pouring himself and his wife a third glass. Eileen took a long time savouring the alcohol in her mouth.

'Mmmm – very good. It must be a good year.' Eileen knew nothing about the quality, vintage or date of birth of wine but she had heard people say that kind of thing before.

'A little more potato or greens, Mother?' she asked.

Lydia would have liked a little more meat and another glass of wine. She shook her head at the prospect of the vegetables but managed to smile. Eileen took Derek's sanction on the drink a little further.

'Blood pressure is something you will always have to watch, Mumsy, and wine or alcohol could affect it. At your age you can't be too careful, you know.' Derek took another sip from his glass and grunted an assent to his wife's sensible rejoinder.

'I've never suffered from blood pressure in my life.' Lydia always tried to avoid any dissent but could not stifle her feelings sufficiently to keep quiet. If they had given her a bit more meat, she might have been able to keep her mouth shut.

Her remark was greeted by stony silence from her son and daughter-in-law. Sometimes Lydia could be very awkward and they had decided that this was the best way to express their disapproval. All their attention was now directed towards their children. All four now proceeded through the Sunday lunch as though Lydia were not present. The elder boy sensed that Granny was being punished and, like the good child he had been brought up to be, he sought to add to it.

'Can we watch the "X" film next time you come, Granny?'

Lydia did not answer him. Eileen let her knife and fork fall on her plate with a clatter and looked meaningfully at her husband. As head of the household, she indicated that some severe strictures were necessary. Derek frowned and addressed the boys.

'Now, lads, you know how your mother and I feel about bedtime. It was very wrong of you to stay up. You knew quite well it would make me angry, and you can see how upset your mother is. Well, there is no visit to the funfair on the Heath this afternoon, and you will be sent to bed at half past six tonight.'

'It was Granny's fault.' The younger boy began to blubber as all the future excitements of the day were shattered. Lydia intervened.

'Derek, really it was my . . . I didn't think . . .'

'Mother, please.' He silenced her.

Lydia's offer to clear the plates away and wash up was firmly rejected by Eileen. Lydia retreated to the lounge, her disgrace resplendent and complete.

'Will you be staying to tea, Mother?' Eileen called from outside the lounge door.

'No, thank you, dear. I should get back as I have some washing to do,' Lydia lied gratefully. Her son entered the lounge and lectured her for ten minutes on the dangers of her coming between – or even ruining the relationships between – him, his wife and his children. Again, he made Lydia feel like a child.

'You are part of the family, Mother, but really, you must try not to interfere. I'll get your case.' These were his last words before he drove her back home.

Eileen pecked her cheek with a kiss and ordered the children to emulate this procedure before Lydia climbed into the car. Lydia felt as though she had been bitten three times.

'See you in a fortnight,' cooed Eileen from the pavement. 'Wave to your grandmother.'

Lydia wound up the car window as the last order was delivered.

2

'*The Kiss*, one of Rodin's most well-known pieces. Its first unveiling caused a great deal of consternation, adulation and opposition. There's nothing sloppy about it, is there? Would you say that it is in any way shocking? It shocked people on its first appearance. This statue is only a copy. The original rests in France.'

'The 'Know Your City' class gathered every Thursday afternoon. It was attended by fourteen senior citizens. They attended diligently as their agency teacher seemed to break all pedagogic rules by presenting a programme that was wide-ranging in the extreme. He often made them laugh. He wore faded blue jeans which were much too tight for his rolypoly figure and short legs. Today he also wore a yellow pullover, and around his neck a chain which held a large, cheaply decorated purple stone. He never bullied or hectored his pupils. Sometimes he shocked them a little; often he made them smile. They found him cheerful, comic and sad, an intellectual version of an ageing music-hall comedian. The officer in charge of the leisure classes did not understand his appeal but never questioned his employment as the attendances for his classes never faltered. If a pupil died, another was soon recruited. Tony Burford was fifty-four. He pranced about as if he were eighteen, and his students called him Bunty.

'They're very big, aren't they? I mean both of them, the man and the woman.' Mrs Batsford always spoke first.

'Well, darling, the sculptor is trying to convey the strength of the theme. Their size and nakedness emphasizes the importance and strength of the action.' Bunty joined in the titters that greeted his response.

'Well, it's better than the *Buggers of Calais*,' said Mr Handley, a rough-tongued, intelligent, retired ironmonger.

'*The Burghers of Calais*, Benny dear. The *Burghers*. They were like city councillors.' Bunty reproved him gently.

'Might as well call them buggers, then, if they were councillors.'

'Be fair, Benny. The councillors approve the grant for our class. Now what would you say is the main quality of this work? Is it passionate, sexy, real? What do you think about it?'

Lydia stroked the great stone elbow of the man, gazed into the silent contours of his grave face, shared the mutual bliss of the silent couple. She had never been held in such a way, never been in bed naked. She had always had to lift up her nightdress or lower the straps, whatever the situation had demanded.

'I think it's very tender, very beautiful. I think that this is how it ought to be. Perhaps them having no clothes on makes it seem not at all rude. It's just natural, isn't it?'

'You stay, please, you stay like that.' A dapper, neat Japanese man had weaved through the small crowd of elderly viewers. He took up his camera and made a swift test as to the suitability of the lighting. Lydia, surprised by his request, took her hand from the stone elbow and clutched her handbag to face the camera.

'Well, I suppose it's all right.' She smiled nervously at the little man.

'No, as you were before, please. As before, please.' The Japanese pointed to the statue and began to adjust his camera lens. Lydia felt a little uncomfortable. Bunty encouraged her to take up her previous stance, so she obeyed him and, before her resolution in the matter had time to weaken, the camera had clicked. The onlookers applauded her courage, and the Japanese man politely took Lydia's address with the promise of sending her a copy of the snapshot in the not-too-distant future.

'I'd like us to have a quick look at some paintings now, just one or two. Those of you who feel you have seen enough can make their way down to the tea bar. It's in the basement. The rest of us will join you in about fifteen or twenty minutes.' Bunty never forced his sense of wonder on his pupils, always aware that a fatigue factor might inhibit some. He dotted his tours and visits with simple but decidely compassionate options. He was not hurt when only three of the number chose to follow him and the rest made their way downstairs for tea and talk.

Lydia lingered behind. She felt she would like the statue to herself for a bit. It would be nice not to have to share it with anyone. She encircled it slowly, her head held back, her eyes fixed on the contours and the spaces between. Finally her stare rested on the man's hands. They were huge. Large enough to cover her own ample bottom.

'Oh, oh, Christ. Oh, my Christ, oh . . .'

Lydia turned sharply. She was not alone. Benny Handley sat on one of the side seats of the gallery. He clutched his chest and began to sway to and fro. Lydia managed to get to him before he fell to the ground. She put her arms about him and held him to her. She looked about her for help but the room was empty. The statues suddenly lost what life they had gained.

'It's my heart. Get my sniffer. It's in my breast pocket.' Benny panted the instructions, and Lydia held the phial to his nose. His breathing became easier but she still felt it necessary to hang on to him. She did not draw away when he kissed the cotton covering of her breasts and stroked and patted her behind.

'There's a good girl. I wish I could get a real hold of you. There's a good girl.' He nuzzled closer into her breast and somehow managed to undo the top button of her dress. She continued to hold him until his breathing became normal. She looked down into his face. He pulled her head towards him. He opened his mouth and she did not resist his tongue as it seemed to push itself into the back of her throat. This was how the gallery attendant found them.

'I could report you for this, you know.' The uniformed man tapped Lydia's shoulder as he spoke.

Benny sat up and did not appear to be at all embarrassed.

'We're just testing positions.' He pointed to the statue. 'It *is* possible to get like that. Try it, it's better than sucking lollipops.' He took Lydia by the arm and leaned on her very slightly. They entered the tea room arm in arm but no one seemed to care too much. Lydia wondered whether they had even noticed. Then, why should they? No, everyone carried on talking.

The senior citizens – or old-age pensioners, as they had formerly been called – did not discuss the works of art they had seen in much detail. This was not to say that they had not enjoyed the afternoon. They always enjoyed the afternoons with Bunty wherever he chose to take them. Over their tea, they talked of their ailments. Legs that were playing up, feet that were crumbling, blood pressure, operations they had recovered from and operations they might have to have in the near future. Their past, present and future perils were interspersed (for the most part) with anecdotes about their children and grandchildren, their cats or their dogs. Some gently complained about the young when they had tired themselves of discussing their own inevitable decay.

'Next week we are visiting Billingsgate. Here are the papers and times and instructions where we are to meet.' Bunty muttered about his group and handed out the information sheets.

'The fish market, oh my God. I was filleting fish half my life,' one of the women half-wailed, half-guffawed.

'Never mind, dear. You've no idea the excitement the place has. It buzzes in more ways than one, I can tell you.' Bunty fingered his pendant, and for a moment it seemed that his thoughts were preoccupied elsewhere. 'I know a man there. A personal contact. He has agreed to show us around. You never know, we might all get a free bit of cod or plaice or something.'

Bunty meticulously checked that all the students knew the meeting-places and made particular arrangements for some people to meet in groups. He bade them goodbye like a butterfly flitting from one to another. A casual observer might have thought him flippant, yet his odd entourage accepted his foibles and were not in any sense unaware of his unstated compassion.

The meetings always ended gently with the students drifting off either alone or in groups. They spent much time in working out the shortest bus routes home in order to use the free transport travel passes the local government had granted them as a reward for their advancing years. They accepted the passes gratefully, not on account of their senility but largely because of their economic circumstance. It was not a question of greed or grab. Pennies had to be watched.

Lydia usually made her way home alone. She liked to stew over what she had seen. However, she was not surprised to find Benny at her side accompanying her along the embankment.

'I like looking at the river.' She spoke first. And thought of the Orinocco and the Amazon, her own rivers. She thought about the statue and of what had happened with Benny in the Tate Gallery. She sat down on an empty wooden bench which faced the river and smiled as the water traffic passed before her eyes. Benny joined her.

'Er, I'm sorry about what happened in the gallery. I'm glad you can laugh about it. I don't know what came over me.' He scratched the few strands of grey hair on his balding head.

'Oh, I wasn't laughing at that, dear.'

'You mean you didn't mind?'

'Didn't mind, Benny? If you had taken a good look at the statue, you ought to know that it takes two to tango. I was just a bit surprised, that's all. No, I can't say that I minded one little bit.' Lydia turned her face from the river and looked directly into his eyes. 'As I say, it was sudden, but now I've had time to think about it a bit more, you might as well know that at the time I enjoyed it.'

'So did I.' Benny took her arm and patted her hand. She made no attempt to resist him. His hands were large, hard and calloused. Lydia felt comforted by the feel of them. In his hands, her own soft pudgy ones felt wanted.

A boat with music blaring from its portholes and young people dancing on the decks passed by. They both sat silent until the noise had passed.

'I had a bad time with Alice, just for the last three years before she went.'

Lydia had never heard Benny refer to his wife before. She felt no resentment, as she felt the need to tell him about her husband, Henry. So their courtship began in exchanges of bereavement. Both of them knew that it was beginning. It was pleasant, much more warm, truthful and tolerant than it was when you were young.

'Well, my Alice always liked a good time, always kept herself smart, had her hair done every week. Weekends we would always go to the club and as often as not she would join in the sing-songs. Sometimes she'd start everybody off. Once or twice she sang on her own over the microphone. But that was only after she'd had a few drinks. To tell you the truth, she hadn't much of a singing voice, loud enough I grant you, but she was never quite in tune. She was a bonny woman, much like yourself. I like bonny women.'

'He likes big tits.' Lydia was pleased with the thought.

'Then she began to make excuses for not wanting to go out. I used to go out for a drink on my own. Then she let the house go. I mean, she would leave things around and not clean. Before then, she'd been spotless. We'd never had any children. Alice's tubes were blocked. Honestly, we never missed them but I wondered if this was why she had become so down in the dumps. She was fifty-three, so it was too late to start a family and too late to adopt. She began to sulk a lot and it got to the point where she would hardly exchange a word with me. Eventually I got her to go to the doctor. He said it was menspores depression.'

'Menopausal depression,' Lydia corrected gently.

'Something like that. He gave her some tablets but they did nothing to ginger her up. Soon she got pernickety about her food and I could see she was losing weight. I made her go to the doctor's again, and this time I went with her. He gave me a ticket and made an appointment for her at the London Hospital in Whitechapel.' Benny sighed.

'When she put on her dress to go for the appointment, I knew there was something wrong. It was one of those dresses for well-made women which buttoned up over one side to give a slim look. Well, it just hung on her like a sack. She didn't seem to care that the buttons were miles out of position. I even had to get some new sets of underwear as she could have got both legs through one of the old pairs of knickers she used to have. She did make an effort, though, on that particular morning. She put some powder and paint on and I persuaded her to have a bit of breakfast before we left. Even through her powder, I could see the veins sticking out on her forehead, and when she chewed or swallowed, her Adam's apple bobbed up and down her throat like a fish float. She had got thin.

'They were nice to us at the hospital. They asked how long she had felt down, and I mentioned that she had had liver trouble five years back. They gave her an X-ray and a blood test and said they would see us again in a week. Alice just nodded. I tried to cheer her up – but she seemed . . .'

'Indifferent,' said Lydia.

'Yes, that's right. You're a clever girl, aren't you?'

Lydia knew that Benny required no answer. He squeezed her hand and continued. He breathed in deeply as though the Thames before him was carrying the ozone of some delightful sea breeze.

'I can always sniff trouble, and it wasn't just the disinfectant smell of the hospital on that second visit. There were two doctors. They had been polite before but this time they were more than polite. They asked me in and even asked a nurse to bring me a cup of tea. I just let the cup stand there. I never drank the tea. It just stood there and went cold.

'"Well, Mr Handley, the investigations and reports on your wife's condition are all completed!"

'"Is she all right?" I asked them. The one that was talking to me didn't look at me directly; the other one did and asked if I wanted a cup of tea or a cigarette.

'I mean, a doctor in a hospital doesn't encourage you to have a fag, these days, does he? Not unless there's trouble. I shook my head and waited for the other one to talk. He spoke slowly and paused a lot.

'"We have made the most thorough checks, and it seems certain that there is something untoward in the condition of your wife's blood."

'"It could be anaemia. She's had liver trouble. Would that be it?" I asked. He didn't waste any time and answered me like rocket fire. I think he wanted to get the news off his chest.

'"Anaemia of a kind, yes, but nothing that vitamins will

cure. You see, Mr Handley, our blood is made up of cells. White ones and red ones, and in your wife's case the white blood cells are rapidly eating up the red ones. I must be frank with you and state that there is nothing we can do to alleviate this situation."

' "What has she got, then?" I do wish he had talked more straight, but he tried.

' "Your wife is in an advanced state of leukaemia. You would call it cancer of the blood."

' "Can't you use the knife – I mean, operate somewhere?" I asked them.

'The doctor who hadn't spoken shook his head, and the other one opened out his hands. Funny, I noticed that he wore a wedding ring. Men don't wear them so much these days, do they?'

'No,' said Lydia. Benny gripped her hand more tightly.

' "Where would we begin to operate, Mr Handley? Your wife's system, her whole body, is riddled with it. I am afraid I have to inform you that your wife is very, very ill, indeed."

' "How ill?" I asked him. This time he looked up from his desk.

' "She is dying," he said.

' "How long?" I asked him.

' "Her condition is advanced. It is difficult to ascertain precisely but I would say between four and six months. I'm sorry." '

Lydia stroked Benny's hand. She respected the matter-of-fact way in which he was reporting the details. Death was matter-of-fact. Lydia had always felt this.

'I never told Alice. I even slept with her. No sex or anything like that. Her hair began to fall out, and eventually it was like lying next to a skeleton. The doctor visited each week and gave her drugs. She didn't seem to be in any pain. She slept a lot. The doctor was right. Just four months later I woke up early. It must have been four in the morning. Her breathing was always gentle but I knew it had stopped. I put my arm over her, just to cuddle her a bit, but she was cold and I knew she was dead.'

'I'm sorry,' said Lydia.

'That was seven years ago. I've never told anyone about it before. At least, not just how it was. I don't think she would mind me telling you. Although, you're not a bit like her. You know, I've forgotten great chunks of our married life together. The last three years weren't much of a life, anyway. I need a woman. I don't like sleeping on my own. It doesn't suit me a bit. I like something to hold onto in the night. Do you know, I put my arm around a pillow in bed each night. I don't try to imagine it's Alice but sometimes when I'm half asleep I believe I'm holding a nice comfortable woman. One like yourself.' Benny loosened his grip on Lydia's hand.

'But you hadn't noticed me until today!' Lydia was curious.

'No, it was the shock. If my dodgy ticker had given out then, I wouldn't have noticed any more. But you were there, and as I came to, I knew I had another innings. I think I noticed your eyes first, and then the rest followed, natural like. It was natural, wasn't it?'

Lydia looked at his face. The lack of hair on his head was compensated by the amount of it that sprouted from his face. Tiny cactus-like sprigs sprang from his nostrils and ears. His eyebrows formed a bush-bar which crossed the bridge of his nose. The eyes were large, light, light blue and clear. In fact, all his features were large. His nose could have been classically Jewish, but it was not unattractive or out of proportion as his mouth was wide and full. Lydia noted with satisfaction that his teeth were his own. She liked the small dent in the middle of his chin. He had nicked his chin whilst shaving, and a tiny spot of congealed blood decorated the side of his attractive dimple. He was of average height, but his shoulders were broad. Long, ape-like arms extended from them. He had the appearance of being a very strong man. Rugged, you might say.

Lydia thought of Clint Eastwood. Then she frowned. How unfair, how cruel it was that Benny's heart did not beat in time with his frame. How sad that the heart just couldn't be wound up like a clock. 'We're ticking all the time, and we have no say at all about the timing . . .' Lydia dwelt on this harsh reflection. She continued to gaze at

Benny. He wasn't over-weight. He certainly wasn't obese. Yes, she liked the look of him. A thrill of sensuous apprehension gurgled within her. But what about the heart? She suppressed a sigh, but shrugged her shoulders.

Benny noticed the gesture and misunderstood it.

'It was stupid of me to think that you fancied me,' he laughed nervously, apologetically. Lydia found this most touching. His humility aroused more subtle passions within her. 'I understand,' he said, turning his eyes from her to look out on the river. 'A woman like yourself would feel sorry for a bloke in that situation. I suppose you must have thought you were giving me the kiss of life.' Gently he released her hand and clasped his own hands together, hunched himself forward and rested his elbows on his knees.

'I don't know whether I fancy you or not, Benny, I was just looking at you, that's all. Perhaps you could give me a little time to make up my mind. After all, it has been all a bit sudden.'

Benny's face creased with relief. He turned towards her and smiled slowly. 'Do you fancy a bit of courting then? I mean, just going places together to see how we get on? Just the two of us.'

Lydia linked Benny's arm with her own and they rose from the seat together.

'Yes, yes, Benny, I fancy a bit of courting. Yes, I'd like that,' she said.

'I'll see you to the bus stop, then.' He spoke as though he were honouring a contract. As they walked along the river's edge, neither of them talked. They paused occasionally on account of Benny's condition. Still, they remained in comfortable silence. Both of them had far too much to think about. There was plenty of time for talking later. Plenty of time.

The late afternoon was warm and soothing. The historic boats (long past voyaging) moored along the Thames were not glimpsed. Lydia and Benny were contemplating a sense of wonder based in the present, not in the past. Not even a keen-eyed, loudly screaming gull broke their reverie. It flew about their heads, settled and perched in front of them and seemed intent on pestering the life out of them. Oblivious to its attention, they strode calmly forward.

3

Barbara, Lydia's eldest child, and her son-in-law Eric had gone out early on the Sunday morning. Lydia was left in the bungalow in Potters Bar with her eighteen-year-old grand-daughter Paula. Barbara and Eric had left in a flurry, giving vague instructions as to what time they were going to return. Paula and Lydia were asked to prepare the Sunday lunch, not cook it. The main foundation of the meal was rice (Barbara tended to have a modern outlook with regard to cooking) so that Paula and Lydia were left with very little to prepare. Barbara had said that if they got hungry they could both nibble at something until she and Eric got back.

Eric had a passion for rose bushes which neither Lydia nor Paula shared. He and his wife were visiting several nurseries in Hertfordshire with the hope of returning with some blooms of an exceptional aroma and distinction of colour that none of their near neighbours could match or rival.

'I think we have too many rose bushes already – forty-four different varieties was the last count. Do you mind if I have a smoke, Gran?' Paula had already taken a cigarette from her packet of ten.

Lydia ignored the question as she knew that Barbara and Eric disapproved of this unhealthy habit their daughter had adopted. If she said nothing to the request, then she could not be accused. One had to be so careful with grand-children. In any event, Lydia loved Paula, who never patronized and often talked with her about things she would never mention to her parents. Lydia enjoyed the confidences and respected them.

In this sense, the weekends in Potters Bar were not as irksome as those spent in Surrey. Barbara and Eric found their daughter Paula 'difficult' and were relieved that Lydia took her off their hands for some of the time. Eric described his daughter as stubborn, and Barbara said she had long given up trying to understand her only child. Lydia found Paula refreshingly honest, perhaps confused, but then who wasn't? Over the past two years she and her grand-daughter had become the closest of friends. It was a strange combination. Some might have considered the depths of their relationship unhealthy, but as only Paula and Lydia plumbed these depths there was no one able to share or comprehend them. Paula puffed at the cigarette whilst Lydia cut and prepared some home-grown runner beans.

'Try a puff, Gran.' Paula held out the half-smoked cigarette. Lydia shook her head.

'No, thanks, dear. I tried it before, when I was much younger. I found the sensation most unpleasant and it is bad for your health. I'm not stopping you, mind. Your life is your own.'

'Grandad never smoked, did he? Who did you try smoking with?'

'Oh, it was a man I was going out with before I met Henry. He was a very unsettled person, and the relation-ship ended when I met your grandfather.' Lydia plopped an operated bean into the colander.

'Did you like him a lot, this other man? Did you like him more than Grandad?'

'Well, he was different, dear. It's quite impossible to compare the two of them. I was very fond of your grand-father.'

Paula stubbed her cigarette, unsatisfied. 'Was he your lover?'

'Good gracious, no. We didn't do things like that in those days. Or at least, some people did but I didn't!'

'You didn't have sexual intercourse before you were married?'

'No, dear, I didn't. I came very close to it, but not quite.' Lydia smiled at the recollection. It had almost happened in the cinema and again inside the doorway of her home. If her father hadn't opened the door at the crucial moment, it would have happened.

'My mother did, didn't she?' Paula replied in a matter-of-fact tone.

'Paula!' Lydia placed the cutting knife on the table, momentarily shocked by her grand-daughter's audacity. Paula picked up the knife and took a turn at slicing the beans.

'She did. She must have done,' said Paula.

'Has your mother discussed this with you, dear? I can't think why you should be thinking of such things.' Lydia was conscious of the fact that her retort was bigoted and postured. Paula's rejoinder did not surprise the older woman.

'Of course she didn't discuss it with me. I wouldn't expect her to. I worked it out for myself. Reckoning my age and the date of the marriage, she was three months pregnant when she married Dad. She was my age. Eighteen.' Lydia flushed.

'You might have been premature, dear,' she said.

'I wasn't though, was I?'

'No, dear,' Lydia finally acquiesced.

'I'm having it myself at the moment.'

'What, dear?'

'Sexual intercourse.'

'Oh?'

'In fact, I've had it with two different people. There are no real restrictions in the hall at the Polytechnic.' (Paula was studying for a degree. Lydia knew that it was something to do with History and Politics but had not ventured to enquire of the intricacies of its content.) 'If the girls wanted to, they could all go absolutely berserk – sexually speaking. But they don't, Gran, really they don't. You could say that what relationships are going on are civilized. There's nobody jumping about from room to room, but some girls have paired with a regular man. Not all of them, just some.'

'You're not having two at a time, dear, are you? I mean you . . . you're not alternating?' Lydia swallowed. She would hate to think of her beloved grand-daughter developing into a nymphomaniac. She tried to present her questions as practicably as possible.

'No, of course not. I'm like a bus conductress. One at a time, please, and no standing upstairs.'

Lydia laughed and replied. 'I don't know what your parents would think.'

'Well, as career teachers, they're both thinking of other children all the time, so the less they think about me the better.' Lydia was sad to note the trace of rancour in Paula's voice.

'Do you want to hear about them?'

'About who, dear?' Lydia was thinking about Benny.

'About my lovers – past and present.'

'Yes, if you like, dear. Shall I finish the rest of the beans while you talk? You might cut yourself if you don't concentrate.'

Paula left the table and looked out onto the serried ranks of rose bushes. Clipped and shorn, they were allowed to produce only three or four blooms. It was a way of preserving the elitism of each flower. Paula often imagined the garden full of wild roses, overgrown bushes that provided dark and secret spaces. In spite of the harshness of her conversation, she was at heart of a romantic nature.

'My first experience of sleeping with a man was the day after my eighteenth birthday. By some girls' standards, you could say that I was a late starter. He was considered by almost all the girls in the college to be the most handsome man in the place. He was studying physics and he played rugby. He was very pleasant and popular. He made people laugh a lot. He told jokes.' Paula turned from the window. Lydia had stopped on the beans.

'Jokes don't make me laugh. That's what I said to him when he just started chatting to me at the discothèque. It seemed to have a terrible effect on him. I thought he was just going to leave me there in the middle of the dance floor. He went so quiet, it affected his animation.'

'I should imagine it would, dear,' said Lydia, who sat agog for more information.

'He asked me if we could go quietly and talk somewhere. We walked across the quadrangle to my hall of residence and went up to my room. The rest of what happened was fairly technical.' Lydia raised her eyebrows questioningly. 'He was very adept, very considerate. Asked me if it was the first time. It happened twice in two hours. I mean, I think he had two orgasms. He called out both times. I can't remember what he said but at least it wasn't glib. While this was going on, I felt as though I were someone else. I suppose it was the excitement of it.

'Afterwards, when we had both calmed down, I waited for him to talk. We might as well have been on the discothèque floor. He started joking again. Silly stories about rugby players, Irishmen, Jews, Blacks and Poofs. I found him revolting. His beauty made it worse. He must have sensed it, because he dried up in the middle of an anecdote.

' "You're not interested in me, are you?"

' "No", was all I said.

'He checked to see if his hair had fallen in the right place over his brow and left. I suppose I should have felt depressed, but I wasn't. As a matter of fact, five minutes later, I was washing my knickers at the sink.'

'How did you feel?' Lydia felt the need to place an arm around her grand-daughter but remained sitting.

'Enlightened', said Paula.

Lydia joined Paula at the French windows. They linked arms.

'The second one is different, isn't he?' Lydia asked gently.

Paula nodded. 'Yes, he's bearded and going prematurely bald and has a slight tendency towards fatness around the belly. His eyes are green and his main interests are football, philosophy and me. I make him laugh a lot, not by telling jokes but just by observing things. There's no direction – or at least there doesn't seem to be any direction – to our relationship. But I don't think about that too much. We have a need to be together all of the time. We are lovers, Gran, lovers. It makes me feel separate.'

Paula led her grandmother into the kitchen. Lydia was about to finish off the last of the beans, but Paula restrained her.

'Gran, do you think that Stephen and me could stay at your house, some weekends? Would you mind if we slept at your place?'

'Together, in one bed?' Lydia asked. It was as though her late husband was talking and not she. She regretted asking the question, but it was too late to withdraw it.

'I didn't want to upset you,' said Paula.

'I'm not upset, my dear. We'll have to work out some sort of plan. I'm afraid we'll have to intrigue a little as there are complications. However, I don't feel averse to offering shelter for lovers.'

Paula kissed Lydia's cheek. 'That's poetic, Gran – shelter for lovers!' Paula exclaimed.

'Is it, dear? It wasn't meant to be. You see, I'm considering taking one myself. It would be hypocritical to deny you what I am contemplating myself.'

Paula gasped, and then let out a great whoop of pleasure. She jumped from her seat and clapped her hands. 'Yippee, yippee!'

Lydia had not expected such a reaction and chose to calm her grand-daughter. 'Shush, dear, shush, shush. I don't want to advertise the fact. It's not the world's business, it's mine. I'm glad you're pleased for me, but don't get carried away. As I've said, there are complications.'

'Your turn, Gran. Who is he? Leave the beans. I knew it would happen.' Paula could not disguise her pleasure.

'You were always perceptive, even as a small child.'

Lydia resigned herself to delivering the facts of her relationship with Benny. Paula waited and listened attentively.

'So you see, the sexual side of things hadn't entered it but now Benny wants it to happen and so do I. But I'm worried about his heart. He is a strong man, he has to be careful, and excessive, undue exertion might kill him. I should hate to contribute towards his death. The thought of killing him with passion horrifies me. It's sad, because I do love him, and, yes, I want him.'

Lydia concluded her story and sighed sadly, deeply, shook her head and looked into the eyes of her grand-daughter for an answer. She did not expect much. How could an eighteen-year-old girl know anything about something so – so – worldly? The dilemma could not be resolved. Lydia misjudged her grand-daughter.

Paula placed her hands on her be-jeaned hips and spoke firmly, almost commandingly. 'There's enough beans out. They won't mind if we eat like sparrows. There's some sherry in the lounge. They've hidden it behind the bookshelf. Come, we're going to have a slug of it together,' Paula ordered. Lydia followed meekly.

After they had consumed three glasses together, Lydia felt a little more carefree, relaxed and, yes, even abandoned. While Paula conducted the extraordinary tutorial, the alcohol helped Lydia to listen and shed fears that were unjust for her to have carried.

'I suppose it was all straight up and down with Grandad. Bang, bang, grunt, grunt, and that was that.' Paula had begun another cigarette.

'Yes, dear, it was a bit like that, but I can't say that I found it altogether unpleasant. No, in all fairness to Henry, it was not altogether unpleasant, although I always hoped for something more. I just don't think it was in his nature, though,' Lydia added ruefully. She did not wish to slander the dead. She thought carefully about what to say next. She frowned, perplexed. She wanted to be truthful.

'Tenderness,' said Paula.

'Yes, that was missing,' said Lydia. 'Although while Henry was carrying on, he was volatile, even violent, at times. He literally exhausted himself on me. It was usually quick, but very intense. I'm sure if Benny carried on in the way Henry had done, the act itself would kill him.' Lydia shook her head and sipped her sherry. 'I really wouldn't want that to happen. I could never forgive myself. It all seems a bit unfair, doesn't it?' Lydia's eyes began to water.

'If you don't mind my saying so, Gran, I think you are being defeatist.' Paula had joined a left wing political group and, without realizing the fact, some of the rhetoric had crept into her ordinary conversation. She repeated the phrase as she topped up her grandmother's glass with more sherry. 'Yes, defeatist!' she declaimed.

'Am I, dear?' Lydia felt as though she were being called a coward.

'You don't think all men go about having it off like Grandad did! If you don't mind my saying so, he sounds like a selfish lover to me. Marjorie Proops or any of those women that write like her could have told you that.'

'Oh, I couldn't write to the papers, dear, not over things

like that.' Lydia was slightly alarmed at Paula's sudden fierceness of tone and abruptness.

'You don't have to. I can get you a book from the library. It gives you details on how to achieve sexual satisfaction in spite of the minor problems you think you and Benny have.'

'Good heavens, do they have books like that in the library? I don't think I would dare ask for one!' Lydia was surprised at the information. Paula noticed the older woman's sense of alarm and addressed her more gently.

'The books come under health, Gran. Health. There are hundreds of positions you can adopt, without Benny killing himself. It might mean you have to do a bit of the love-making and not just lie back. It has illustrations.'

Lydia felt bewildered. Paula was a sensible girl, but . . .

'In fact, if you don't go to bed with Benny, it will be bad for your health and his. Yes, bad,' said Paula.

'I think you're right, dear.' Lydia finished her sherry bravely.

'Good. I'll get the book for you and bring it round.'

'If you wouldn't mind,' said Lydia, her head spinning with the thought of hundreds of positions. Surely, three or four would be enough – comfort was the main thing.

Both women heard the car backing into the garage. Paula pushed the sherry bottle behind the volumes of the *Encyclopaedia Britannica*, and Lydia hastened to wash the glasses in the kitchen. Paula opened a textbook entitled *The Sanity of Madness* and Lydia resumed finishing off the last of the beans.

'I hope you're not starving.' Barbara started speaking before removing her anorak. Eric wore one of an identical colour. He kept his on as he held a plastic sack close to him with great care as if it were a new-born baby.

'Did you nibble anything? It's late, I know, but we've seen some lovely varieties. We just went from one to another. It was impossible to resist them, and the time just ticked away.' Barbara was having some trouble with the zipper on her anorak as she spoke.

'It usually does tick,' said Paula.

'What?' Barbara half-snapped at her daughter.

'Time,' said Paula.

Barbara ignored her daughter and spoke to her mother. 'Oh, Mother, don't you think roses are miraculous? So English in their way.'

Lydia could not follow her daughter's train of thought and looked at her in a puzzled fashion. Lydia hoped the sherry wasn't affecting her head. Barbara explained.

'They always say you can never tell an Englishman abroad because we all look so different. Our hair, pallor, eyes, height, all so variable.' Barbara had managed to get her anorak off. Her gushing irritated Paula, but she kept quiet.

'Er, er, er-m, you can usually identify English people by their clothing – at least, a certain group or class of English person. I've picked them out in France and Italy, and I didn't have to speak to them.' Eric was hoping for an argument or discussion. He enjoyed stimulating conversation. Both he and Barbara were teachers and tended to have controlled domestic differences on facts which most people would not bother to discuss. As a very happily married couple, they always smiled at each other through these mindless, intellectual disagreements. Paula hated them.

'I suppose English people wouldn't need passports if they travelled naked, then.' Paula did tend to punish her parents. She was hungry. It was half past three. Lydia tittered at her grand-daughter's remark.

'Paula, there's no need to be flippant or rude. If you've nothing sensible to say, keep quiet,' Barbara hissed at her daughter. 'I'll heat up the curry. Lunch should be ready by four. Could you place the rose bushes in water, Eric? We'll plant them after the meal before it gets dark. These blooms re-a-ll-y are astonishing, Mother. Wait till you see them.' Barbara's face took on an anguished expression as she paused for a few seconds bucolic reflection. 'How people can ever cut them from their natural setting and place them in a vase, I shall never know. Then, any form of cruelty is quite beyond me.' Barbara left the lounge for the kitchen, and Eric departed to impart a good half of the nurture he possessed into his roses.

'They should never have had children,' said Paula. Lydia did not argue but mused. The sherry had affected her a little.

'I like to see roses about the house. Even when they are fading a little. The fallen petals always look so attractive.' Lydia had never received a single bloom from her daughter. It had never entered Lydia's head that by putting flowers in a vase you were murdering them. No, it couldn't be murder – and Barbara had so many of them, just three or four that were not special would have been so nice on the table near the window.

'I'll nick some for you before you leave, Gran.'

'What, dear?'

'I'll steal a bunch of their bloody roses.'

'Now, I don't want to cause any trouble, dear. I don't want you to suffer on my account. Darling, you must try to be a little more discreet with your parents.'

'I'll suffer if I don't steal them.' Paula spoke defiantly.

Lydia shook her head. There was no doubting the fact, Paula was a determined girl, but she had to be. Lydia had always felt that her daughter and son-in-law had ignored rather than neglected their only child. Poor Paula was like an addendum; she was the postscript of a perfectly natural function. Ever since her arrival, Paula had always been a bit in the way. True, she was well fed and clothed, but Eric and Barbara had always liked to plan. Paula had not been planned and, unlike the rose bushes, she needed more than water and manure in order to blossom. However, in spite of the detached care her parents had preferred, Lydia found her grand-daughter appealing and – yes – beautiful in her way.

'You're sure you don't mind, Mother?' Barbara sweetly asked. Lydia was rather tired and the thought of the long journey home did not exactly leave her excited. Nevertheless, Lydia succumbed her own fatigue to the after-care that Barbara and Eric could extend to the roses.

'No, dear, of course I don't mind. I can catch the 29 bus all the way to Finsbury Park,' said Lydia.

'You could get home quicker if you broke the journey and

travelled part of the way by tube.' Eric had begun to clear away the lunch crockery.

Paula left the room. Her parents' insensitivity never surprised her but in order to avoid a scene which might upset Lydia she escaped into the garden. She returned five minutes later clutching a plastic bag. Barbara was helping Lydia on with her coat.

'I'll walk you to the bus stop, Gran,' said Paula. Eric glanced at the plastic bag.

'They're runner beans. You mentioned in the week that we might give some to Gran. The deep freeze is blocked out with them as it is, and there's still lots more beans on the plants.' Paula slung her coat about her shoulders.

'I'm sure you'll enjoy them, Mother. You can't beat garden vegetables.' So saying, Barbara pecked Lydia on the cheek, and Eric patted her shoulder.

'See you soon,' they both chorused.

Lydia watched the red bus round the bend and turned to her niece as it made its way towards them. 'I shan't change onto the underground. I'll go all the way by bus,' she said.

'I would, if I were you. Can I call around and see you next week?' Paula asked.

'Come on Saturday, dear. I'm not going to Surrey. No, I'm not going to Surrey,' said Lydia in a most decided fashion, and added, 'I'm changing my routine.'

Paula grinned at this gesture of gentle family disobedience. 'Oh, good, good, Gran. I'm so glad.' She threw her arms about Lydia and embraced her. Vapours of Lily of the Valley ascended her nostrils. The bus arrived.

'Hurry along, please.'

Lydia stepped onto the platform, and Paula thrust the plastic bag into her hands.

'Your beans, your runner beans. Saturday, Saturday!' she called after the receding bus.

Lydia waved and climbed the iron stairs for a seat on the top of the bus. The tops of buses tended to be less crowded and, if one chose, one could see much more.

She showed the conductor her free travel pass. The bus was almost empty, so he had time to be human.

'You look good for your age,' he said, his black, middle-aged face beamed approval. Lydia felt better already. The conductor left her to place her pass back in her purse. She transferred her purse to her handbag and then decided to put the handbag inside the plastic one. She liked to have her hands free. She almost cried out with the pain as a sharp, stabbing sensation hit the side of her hand as she plunged it into the bag. She withdrew her hand quickly and cautiously peered into the plastic bag.

'Naughty girl, naughty girl,' thought Lydia as she stared at the roses. She broke into a gurgle of private pleasure and laughter. A spottle of blood trickled from the side of her hand. She licked it and sucked at the wound. It tasted warm, salty. Lydia continued to lick it long after it had stopped bleeding. She had tasted blood, her own blood. It made her feel very much alive.

4

'It's alive! My God, it's alive! Benny, Benny!' Lydia screamed out. She stared in horror as the long, black, shiny eel began to crawl and squirm its way across the smooth laminated table top. Perhaps it was just nerve endings keeping the body moving. Lydia peered at it. The creature's eyes were open and, as if to justify its point, it opened its jaws and gasped.

'Oh, Benny, Benny! It's alive!' She was relieved to hear the lavatory flush and even more relieved when he joined her in the kitchen of his terraced home.

Lydia had decided she was ready for new experiences. The visit to Billingsgate Fish Market had brought its rewards to the senior citizens. They had left with a piece of cod or bits of plaice for their evening meal.

In spite of the smell, the market had been exciting. Lydia had marvelled at the busyness and confusion of the place. The workers themselves were kind and friendly. As for the bad language, well, it just seemed to come to all of them naturally. There was no venom behind it. Lydia thought that in all probability it was worse to say 'Blast you' to someone than 'Fuck you.' It all depended on the delivery. She had agreed to eat with Benny that evening. He had chosen an eel because she said she had never tasted it. She looked at the squirming creature, her appetite fast dissolving.

'You go and sit yourself down in the front room.' Benny seized the eel by the back of the neck and withdrew with it to the scullery. 'It's not how things look but how they taste that matters,' he called out.

Lydia sat where she was, not quite convinced by Benny's assurance. She heard two heavy thumps come from the scullery. Benny said 'There!'

'He's cut the creature's head off,' thought Lydia.

Benny called out to her once again. 'You would feel the

same way about a rabbit if it was hopping about the garden. Go and sit in the front room and I'll join you when I've put this to stew in some parsley.' Parsley sounded more civilized and Lydia concentrated her thoughts on that sober plant and did as she was asked. After all, when you ate a rabbit you didn't think about its ears, or its whiskers, or its nervous, twitchy nose. Lydia was too truthful about her enjoyment of flesh to be hypocritical about eating it. Still, she wished she hadn't seen the creature squirm.

Lydia settled herself on the large settee which was part of what was formerly called a three-piece, moquette-covered suite. It consisted of two enormous chairs and a large couch covered in hard-wearing cloth. It had a flowered pattern on it, mainly pink and green. The colours were now somewhat faded. This gave the furniture (which took up almost the whole room) a comfortable look about it. It was comfortable. Lydia reclined on the settee, which could easily have accommodated four people in sitting positions. She had it to herself. She lay back with her head on one of the massive arm rests, slipped off her shoes and placed a couple of cushions under her feet. According to medical instructions this posture of having her legs higher than her torso would help relieve the strain on her varicose veins. Lydia had now adopted it each day from habit, not from faith in the advice.

Advice was suspect even if it was self-inflicted. Look at the way things were going between Benny and herself. Sitting on the embankment she had imagined or advised herself to enter a slow and quietly revealing courtship with Benny which might have culminated finally in a consoling friendship based on their mutual loneliness. She had planned to see him once or, at the most, twice a week for the first two or three months. It hadn't been like that at all. He had telephoned her on Sunday and they had spent every day after that in each other's company. They had done quite a bit of kissing and cuddling which Lydia had felt no inclination to resist. He had asked her to stay the night with him on Wednesday but she had declined. It was an unselfish gesture on her behalf as Benny seemed most urgent and, what is more, she felt urgent. But what about his heart? Lydia had not had much training in actual sexual skill; if they both got carried away . . . Lydia had left him most reluctantly. He loved her perfume. He had told her so and, what is more, he had kissed her fleshy thighs and enthused over them. Henry had never done that.

Lydia let flip her suspender tops. They tended to come to life towards the end of the day and, unless she released them, they left ugly red weals on the tops of her legs. It was a long time since she had felt so relaxed. She closed her eyes.

'Fancy dreaming about babies,' thought Lydia. She had half-woken from her slumber with the distinct sensation that she was suckling her first baby. It had been such a long time ago, and Lydia did not dream. If she did, she never had any memory of it. The sensation was so pleasant, the dream so sweet, that she closed her eyes once more in order to recapture it. She knew it would be fleeting – dreams were. It was only after she had closed her eyes that she realized two things. One, that she was quite conscious and not dreaming. Two, that the mouth and tongue which was sucking, fluttering and darting about her left breast did not belong to a baby.

'No need to panic. Perhaps I'll just keep my eyes closed and be still.' Her other breast now was being fondled, stroked, its size encompassed by a large hand which squeezed it gently and intermittently fingered its nipple. It was quite impossible to feign sleep now. Lydia opened her eyes, feeling much more distinctly aware and awake than she had for years.

Benny was kneeling at her side. He was quite naked. Most of his body was covered with tiny, fluffy hairs. Henry hadn't had hairs on his chest, let alone his shoulders. Yet this great, bearlike man was handling her, eating her as though she were the most delectable morsel on earth. He must have been very quiet, very delicate, very gentle about it all, Lydia thought, as she took stock of her own position.

Her dress (which had buttons right down its middle) was unbuttoned and laid wide open on either side of the settee. Her stockings, knickers and bra lay in a heap on the floor beside her. She too was naked. Benny, sensing that she was aroused gave her no time for any more reflection. He kissed her mouth, her eyes, and explored the inside and back of her ears with his tongue. All of these actions were slow and his hands continued to caress.

'Let's lie on the rug,' he half commanded her.

Lydia responded by stroking his shoulders and slid off the couch, willingly, to join him on the carpet. Everything happened slowly. There was so much kissing, so much fondling. Benny appraised Lydia's body as though it were a hymn. He kissed and licked her in a place that Henry had used like a sink that had to be unblocked by force. Benny opened her, made every part of her feel wanted. She responded as best she could, touching him and murmuring unheard-of things which had lain dormant in the recesses of her mind.

'Now, Benny, do it now,' Lydia sighed.

There was no pain. Again, it was slow. His hands kneaded her buttocks. She gasped with pleasure as he climbed across her and eased himself into her.

'Can you feel it? You've got it all, now,' he whispered into her ear.

'Mmmm-mmm.' Lydia clasped him to her.

'Tell me when you're ready,' he said some minutes later.

'Now, now, now,' Lydia cried. He quickened his activity and called out.

'You have it now; it's coming, hold it, hold it.'

Lydia could not do anything else, as she had reached climactic proportions which she had never known existed.

They lay for a while on the rug, side by side. He held her hand and stroked her hair, kissed her occasionally on the neck and breast. He spoke first.

'That was good, lovely. Did you enjoy it?'

'Yes.' Lydia lay inert, relaxed beyond the point of sleep but quite awake. The sensation was new to her. She sighed and touched him between his legs. He was small down there now.

'It was very nice, Benny, very nice,' she said.

'I'll make a cup of tea; then we can eat later. They're better if they stew slowly.'

'What?'

'Eels,' he said.

'I won't be needing that book,' said Lydia.

'Book?' Benny was puzzled but didn't pursue the investigation of Lydia's thoughts. He left her to dress and departed to examine his stew.

Lydia picked up bits of her clothing and dressed carefully. Techniques, what rubbish. All you needed was someone to help you like your own body – no, love your own body, as well as theirs. The rest followed. Lydia pulled on her knickers and admired own plump thighs. She stroked them with great satisfaction before she put the rest of her coverage in place. Benny called out, informing her that the meal was ready. She glanced in the mirror, put on a little powder, another dab of scent, fluffed her hair and hastened to join him. The proceedings that had gone before had given her an appetite. Was love supposed to do that too?

'Dip your bread in the sauce. Don't waste the sauce. Pick the flesh up with your fingers and suck it off the bone. There's no small bones, just one large central one. All the flesh around it is good.' Benny cajoled her to eat. She had picked up the spoon and laid it down twice as she looked at the lumps of flesh floating in the pale green sauce on the plate before her eyes. Benny had already begun to eat.

She seized a lump of eel with her fingers and sucked at it quickly as though it were medicine which was vile-tasting but good for her. To her surprise she liked the taste. Benny tore off a chunk of bread and passed it to her.

'Dip, go on, dip.'

Lydia found his gesture biblical. She copied him and ate with her hands. The spoon and fork remained obsolete at the side of her plate.

'It's delicious,' she said, her mouth half full of food.

'At one time, you could buy them for next to nothing. Expensive now, though. Seems there's no call for them, not enough people want them. Those that do have to pay quite a lot. I suppose it's a dish for – er –'

'Connoisseurs,' said Lydia.

'Is that French?'

'Half and half, I think,' said Lydia.

'How can you have a word half French and half English?

I've never heard of one before. Prove it, and you'll get something special.'

'Café,' said Lydia.

'Yes, I've heard of that. You're very clever.'

'Nobody has ever said that to me before,' said Lydia and sucked at a succulent lump of eel. Admiration was a new experience, particularly pleasing when so sincerely delivered.

Lydia glanced at her watch and immediately wished she hadn't. That sort of action always lets the other person know that you wanted to leave. She didn't, and did not wish to give Benny any false impressions. However, she stood and patted his shoulder.

'Now, I must be on my way. It's past nine. Before I go, I'm doing the washing-up. You did the cooking.'

He smiled and nodded, and watched her clear away the plates. Lydia's task was simple, for his scullery was clean and orderly, all the utensils kept in perfect order. She dried her hands on the towel and came back to join him. He had collected her topcoat and handbag from the hall. He helped her on with her coat and as he did so gripped her shoulders gently.

'Are you sure you don't want to stay? Stay the night. I mean just for comfort,' he spoke quietly.

Lydia remained with her back to him and eased herself closer towards his chest. They stayed like that for a while. Lydia put her arms behind her so that they half encircled his waist.

'I promised to look in on Mrs Thackray. She lives two doors down from me. She's eighty-one, very independent. She has a home help call in the day to tidy up for her and get her a meal. Otherwise, I don't think she would eat. I call in of a night just to check up on things. She's forgetful and a bit confused. Once she had left a saucepan on the stove: I don't know what she was boiling. The place was full of smoke. The saucepan had boiled dry and was white hot. Another time she had fallen asleep in front of the gas fire. If she had fallen forward . . . I just check up, that's all. Do you know she calls me by different names? Sometimes she calls me Mary, sometimes Dorothy, once I was Aunty Grace.

Last night she called me the "White Angel". I couldn't, for the life of me, think why because I was wearing this frock, which is red.' Lydia paused. 'Otherwise, Benny, yes, oh yes, I would like to stay for the comfort. You do understand, don't you?'

'Yes, you should go. But you will stay over sometime soon?'

She turned to him. 'As soon as possible,' she said.

'I'll telephone you tomorrow, as usual.' He escorted her to the door and was about to kiss her farewell. 'Oh, I nearly forgot something. Wait a minute.'

Lydia lingered on the doorstep. He came back with a small unwrapped cardboard package.

'I couldn't read the name,' he said. 'I had one hell of a time sniffing all of the bottles in the chemist. None of the names on the bottles were in English. It is the right one, isn't it? It is the scent you wear? My head is full of it. I can sniff it even after you've gone. It's as though you leave a bit of you behind with me. I like that.'

Lydia looked at the package, overcome by his kindness. Damn Eileen and her lectures on heavy perfume.

'Yes, Benny, this is my scent. It's written in French. It says "Lily of the Valley", but this,' Lydia held up the package. 'This is the best quality. I've never had such good quality as this before.'

Lydia placed the Yale key reluctantly in Mrs Thackray's front door. It opened easily – a child could have opened it with a hair-pin. Mrs Thackray had long gone past the stage of being frightened by intruders and had resisted pressures on having a second, more substantial lock added. 'I've always had my front door open,' she would say. Lydia closed the door quietly behind her.

'You'll be Mrs Poulton.' Lydia was greeted by a woman of about forty, dressed in a green tweed costume. She stood in the hallway, and it was clear that she intended Lydia to go no further. She extended a gloved hand which shook limply. 'I'm Mrs Leverton, Dorothy Leverton, Mrs Thackray's daughter. We've never met. The people next door have explained how very kind you have been to Mother over the past two years – so I waited for you to call. I had to make my way up from Hampshire. We live in the country, you know. What with the journey and the shock of the news, I'm quite worn out.'

'I'm pleased to meet you,' Lydia said.

'Yes, Mother died in her sleep. Possibly in the early hours of the morning. Who knows? The social services department telephoned me at 10.30 a.m. and I've been here ever since three this afternoon. I suppose it's a blessing really.'

'What?' asked Lydia.

'Mother passing over, I mean. For the past five years I've never felt that she had the will to live. Now she's at rest and, although we shall miss her, in all truth, I'm glad her time is complete.'

Lydia swallowed hard. She did not want to cry in front of this businesslike lady. How would she know that her mother had lost the will to live? She hadn't bothered to see her for years. Anger surged through Lydia. If she had been able to speak, she might have shouted out one of the obscene remarks she had heard in the fishmarket. Instead, she began to sob and blubber.

'Sometimes she would call me by your name – Dorothy, Dorothy, she would say and . . .' Lydia's response was blocked by grief and tears.

'It must be upsetting for you.' The woman took Lydia by the elbow and guided her back to the front door. 'I've made all the arrangements necessary, so please don't trouble yourself any more. Mother wouldn't have liked you to be upset. I know that.'

'You know nothing of the kind, you cold, heartless bugger,' thought Lydia as she entered the night air.

'Oh, Mrs Poulton,' the woman called after her. Lydia, already stricken, found it hard to turn around. She stood still and waited for the woman to come to her side. 'The key?'

'Pardon me?' Lydia asked.

'The key to the door, dear. You won't be needing it any more.'

Lydia passed it over without comment. Not glancing at

the woman, she averted her eyes and walked away from her as quickly as she could.

Lydia placed two pillows on her bed that night. She needed Benny lying next to her – it was too late to telephone him now. She was sharply reminded of the imminence of his death. Perhaps this was why she was breathing so heavily. Perhaps this was why she felt the waves of love and intensity which shook her as she thought of him. She kept his image fixed in her head, willed him to stay alive, and slept.

5

'It sounds daft to me. Staying with your Granny when we can just as well stay at your room. It's daft, Paula.'

Stephen Armitage carried the suitcase, nonetheless, as he and Paula walked around the corner to enter the top end of the street. Paula ignored him. She had already explained why she wished to stay at Lydia's. The room at college where they slept together was small, the single bed adequate for passion but not for comfort. Stephen came from Wolverhampton and he tended to lapse into his Midlands accent when he was irritable. Normally, he would not have used the word 'daft'.

He was twenty-eight, older than most men at the Polytechnic. His arrival there had been inadvertent. On leaving school at sixteen, he was without academic qualifications. This was not entirely the fault of his teachers at the comprehensive school. He had not (during his school days) had the slightest interest in learning. His spare time was spent playing football and he got through his secondary school years with the minimum amount of effort with regard to any of the basic subjects. He was an intelligent boy but, as one of the teachers had written on his last report, he 'lacked motivation'. In spite of his cursory attitude towards ambition, he had been quiet, unproblematic and well liked.

It wasn't until he was twenty-three years of age that boredom struck him harshly and fiercely. He still played football but was now one of the oldest members of the side. The evenings were empty. There had been girls, three or four, but after having them he felt guilty that there wasn't much more in it than that for him. They were nice girls and he had felt rotten about dropping all of them. If the evenings were empty, the days reached a pitch of boredom which he felt might eventually affect his sanity. The evening classes stopped him visiting a psychiatrist, and for the next three years he studied in a private, secretive way which gave him an almost criminal satisfaction. It was as though he were cheating the firm where he worked as a sales-ledger clerk, cheating his mother, cheating the whole of Wolverhampton. He continued with his football and substituted his past girl-friends with masturbatory fantasies of some girl who would pop out of his examination results. Everyone but Stephen was surprised when he was informed that he had passed eight 'O' levels and three 'A' levels. His achievement was held to be miraculous by the evening institute and they felt proud of him. His mother was astonished when he quietly gave her the results. Two months later she was physically sick when he informed her he was leaving home to attend a Polytechnic in London.

'You have a steady job. I don't know why you can't settle down with a nice girl like everyone else!'

He did not know either, so it was in some state of confusion that at twenty-six he left his comfortable home to enter a degree course in Sociology and Economics. Even after he had arrived in London and begun the course, the motivation was still a bit of a mystery to him. But there was a football team and within three months he had met Paula. Motivation did not seem to worry her.

'I hope you're not going to start sulking. We're nearly there,' she said.

'I'm not,' he said.

Stephen had a habit of going quiet for long periods. Sometimes Paula would challenge his silences, but on the whole she respected them. He liked her for that. She was a problem, in that he liked her too much. He hated being away from her. He wanted her within touching distance of him all the time. They had quarrelled about his possessiveness and uncalled-for jealousy of any minor relationships she might attempt to establish. Stephen was all for the emancipation of women but Paula was the only thing on earth he desired to own. She responded to his affection. Apart from the physical side of their relationship, he placed upon her a constant emotional and social demand. An upbringing of total intellectual consideration without any trimmings had never brought such demands Paula's way. She accepted them willingly.

'That's the house, the one with the tree outside. It's number twenty-five.' Paula paused and pointed to the tree, and Stephen changed the suitcase to his other hand.

'What's she like?' he asked.

'Who? Gran? She's cuddly, wears quite a lot of make-up. Has her hair soft-permed once a fortnight and reads sexy books. She hides them when people are about. My mum and dad and Uncle Derek and Aunt Eileen all think she's common. They never have her round if they have friends in. They refer to her as Blossom when she's not with them.'

'Why?'

'She wears a lot of scent. Always has, always will. I like her more than anybody. She is incapable of . . .'

'What?'

'Incapable of bad thought. Incapable of bad thought of any kind,' said Paula.

'Now I *am* nervous,' said Stephen.

The introductions were not difficult. Lydia did not seem at all ill at ease. Paula was surprised to find her grandmother dressed in her best finery. Stephen found the old lady comfortable and accommodating.

'I've bought some French bread, ham and tomatoes. Afterwards there's a nice chocolate sponge cake. I baked it myself this morning. Shall I put the kettle on? Yes, I will. Young people are always hungry, although most of them seem so thin nowadays. Young men and young girls were – or seemed to be – bigger when I was young. But being buxom was fashionable then.' Lydia smiled at Paula. 'It looks as though you have taken after me, dear,' she said.

Stephen smiled slowly for the first time. He liked Paula's large bosom, and her pear-shaped bottom was even sweeter out of jeans than squeezed into them.

'Gran! I'm not fat,' Paula cried.

'Oh no, dear, no, no you're not. Nobody could ever say that but you are well made. Like I say, you look a lot like I did when I was a young girl.' Lydia set out the table for two. Paula was puzzled.

'Aren't you eating with us, Gran?'

'Er, er, no, dear, I'm not. I'm eating elsewhere a little later,' said Lydia, as she poured out cups of tea for Paula and Stephen. She turned to him. 'Sugar?'

'Two, please.'

'Good, you've got a sweet tooth. That means you'll enjoy the cake.' Lydia fluttered around the table. Paula had not touched her tea or ham.

'Gran, sit down,' she said.

'Yes, I will now, dear. Everything's ready. Everything's finished.' Lydia sat at the far end of the table.

'I've got that book for you. It's in my bag. Shall I get it?' Paula stared fixedly at Lydia, who chose not to meet her gaze but answered her and spoke to Stephen.

'I won't be needing it, dear – is the ham all right? It's off the bone.'

'Lovely,' he said.

'What time are you leaving?' Paula asked.

'In about ten minutes. You know where everything is, don't you?'

'Yes. What time will you be back?'

'Oh, don't wait up for me, dear. The two of you mustn't wait up for me. Perhaps I will have a cup of tea after all.'

Lydia left for the kitchen and returned with a cup and saucer. Paula poured out her tea.

'We are used to staying up late, Mrs Poulton, very late. We've brought a cassette with us, so we'll be listening to music.' Stephen wanted to sound considerate.

'We are not going to bed until you get back, Gran. Really, there's no need to be creeping about your own house and trying to imagine we are not here. If you feel upset about our staying the night, then say so. We are going to wait until you come back before we retire. You must face up to things, Gran.' Paula stirred her tea vigorously.

'For just a moment, dear, you sounded like your mother.' Lydia sipped her tea.

'I've gone too far,' thought Paula, who felt wretched.

'As a matter of fact, if you decide to wait up for me, you may become very tired. You see, I'm not returning until tomorrow morning, somewhere around 11 a.m.' Lydia stood and smoothed her dress.

'You're not going to Aunt Eileen's, not going to Mum's and . . .'

'As I've said already, Paula, I do not need that book,' said Lydia.

'Oh, Gran, I'm so glad,' said Paula.

Lydia did not feel the need of Paula's enthusiasm or euphoria. She was a little embarrassed by it. It was as though her grand-daughter were encouraging her in some sort of excess that she was not entitled to. Of course, Paula didn't mean it that way, but that was how it felt. Lydia was one of those people who did not need social training or the inculcation of rules of etiquette. Politeness had always come to her naturally. In this matter, she and Paula were not altogether alike. Lydia sought to draw the attention away from herself.

'I like your beard, Stephen. It's very striking. Your hair must have been quite blonde when you were a child. There are still strands of it left. I can see the streaks here and there. That's what makes your beard look so dramatic. It's dark brown, quite a different colour from the hair on your head. It does suit you.'

Stephen was pleased with Lydia's appraisal. He had expected a formula of family questions from her: 'Where are you from? How long is your course? What are you studying? What do you intend to do when you have finished your study?' He had dreaded them coming, and much to his surprise and delight Lydia had not gone in for the usual personal autopsy that parents and relatives inflict on lovers. Instead, she had chosen only to admire his beard. Like many men he had grown it to draw attention away from the beginnings of his premature baldness, which worried him at times. Sometimes Paula would push his hair away from his forehead and examine his receding hairline, and coldly state the number of years he could hope for, before he was left with wisps at the side. He was not vain but such actions as this (although they were delivered in tenderness) hurt him. He did not enjoy his advancing state of baldness. Lydia had admired his beard and he grinned with satisfaction – at least that was not going to fall out.

'This is very good of you, Mrs Poulton, to let us have the

house like this. It's difficult to be private at college. There are always people knocking on the door wanting to tell you something, or borrow something. It's not private there at all,' he said.

'I can imagine,' said Lydia, putting her coat on and clamping down the clasps on her small weekend case. 'Although, really, Stephen, you have nothing to thank me for. I don't like the idea of leaving the house empty for weekends. Houses weren't built to be left empty, were they? I mean, an unused building is useless, isn't it, unless it's a work of art? But even then, it ought to be used, yes, even then,' said Lydia.

'You think all art should be utilitarian, then, Gran?' Paula asked.

Lydia did not understand her. And, in order not to show her ignorance in front of Stephen, she pretended not to hear Paula's question but pursued her own train of thought.

'Yes, I was thinking how dreadful it is to leave this house vacant each weekend. For the future, for the indefinite future, I shall not be staying here on Friday, Saturday or Sunday evenings. I was wondering if the two of you would care to look after the place for me?'

Paula's jaw fell a little. She had not expected her grand-mother to be quite so decisive as this.

'We'd like to, we'd like to very much. Thanks,' said Stephen, who felt quite at home.

'There'll be complications, Gran. What about the shuttle service between Surrey and Hertfordshire?' Paula sounded apprehensive.

'That's going to end, dear. To be truthful, it's ended as from now. I'll let them know gradually. I'll find excuses for the first few weeks and see if they will accept the fact that I have been weaned,' said Lydia.

'What a nice way of putting it,' said Paula. 'They won't accept it, though,' she added.

'I'll face all that when it comes,' said Lydia.

'Look at the roses you gave me, dear. They're still fresh, still open.' Lydia breathed deeply. 'What a lovely aroma they leave around.'

Stephen could smell flowers but the scent was heavier than that of roses. 'They smell lovely,' he lied.

'What's his name?' Paula had accompanied Lydia to the door.

'Benjamin, but I call him Benny. He's a retired iron-monger.'

'Can I meet him?'

'I'd rather like to keep him to myself,' said Lydia. 'It's a long time since I have not had to share; no, darling, I'm keeping him to myself. Well, I'll see you tomorrow and we can work out future arrangements.'

'You can trust me, Gran.'

Stephen waved goodbye, and Lydia gripped her case and left.

'I think your Granny is very attractive. Quite sexy,' said Stephen, after the door had closed.

'Do you really?' asked Paula.

'Yes.'

Paula was amazed by the frankness of his reply and then felt strangely proud. It wasn't everybody that could boast of having a sexy Granny. Paula began to laugh and Stephen laughed with her, not quite knowing what was supposed to be funny.

6

The community hall was bedecked and garlanded with decorations that stretched from rafter to rafter. Blue and red paper balls hung from the lights. Gold and silver stars, carefully threaded on cotton, formed window decorations. The small lights blinked on and off on the fir tree which stood in the corner of the platform stage. Long trestle tables were decorated with holly-leaf motif paper covers. Sixty plates containing turkey, sprouts, roast potatoes and stuffing were placed before the assembled company of categorized aged. It was Christmas.

At least, it was 21 December, which was the most convenient day near to Christmas when the local residents' association could make their goodwill gesture towards their elderly counterparts. Anyone sixty or over and retired could apply. Bunty had passed on five passes to members of his 'Know Your London' group. In order not to offend him, Benny and Lydia had accepted a pass each. They sat together, now, looking at the meal set before them. As each pensioner had entered the hall, they had been ushered (some even led) to their allocated seats. The passes were numbered. It was a well-organized occasion for people who had in one way or another been organized for most of their lives.

'Don't begin until the music starts,' a fresh-faced young woman called from the platform, and clapped her hands. 'Jingle bells, jingle bells . . .' The music played, and the seated company took up their knives and forks and began to eat.

In spite of their years, they ate quickly – a good meal was not to be sniffed at, particularly if you didn't cook it for yourself. Some of them would have liked to talk a little, but the music was very loud and the warm-hearted lady helpers were carried away by their own goodwill and shouted across the tables to one another. Whereas children might have made the party their own with some spontaneous form of anarchic play, the elderly accepted the fact that they were being fed and humoured. The main course was followed by Christmas Pudding and then mince pies and a cup of tea. Lydia resisted the mince pies but drank her tea. She placed her hand on Benny's knee. He covered it with his own. She sighed, 'Thank God it's over.' Now they could escape.

Her expectations were short-lived. The helpers descended like locusts and cleared the tables. No one sitting was allowed to help. They were commanded to remain seated.

An Old Tyme Music Hall had been organized for a follow-up. There were three performers. A man of about thirty-five or forty opened the proceedings by playing a medley of songs on a banjo. Lydia did not find this unpleasing as she had not heard the instrument played for years. Unfortunately, he went on for too long and before his sixth and closing melody was finished it was hard to catch the tune as the seated company had lost interest and begun to talk to one another. The helpers clapped him loudly, and the captive audience was shushed into silence by the fresh-faced lady in charge who announced a lady soprano.

A very large lady in a sparkling turquoise dress smiled benignly at her audience, challenging them to speak one word before she let out a single chord. She sang three songs, all of them sad, all of them received in silence, so that she hardly took a breath before one followed another. 'Just a Song at Twilight', 'Love's Last Word is Spoken' and 'Roses of Picardy' were all delivered to an audience who now felt more dead than alive. The artist received reverent applause, and some of the folk murmured that she had a good, strong voice. All three songs had increased Lydia's depression.

'Can we go, Benny?' He nodded. They made as if to rise but, before Lydia could step behind her chair a bright, chirpy voice and a tap on her shoulder caused her to turn her head sharply.

'You want the toilet, dear?'

Lydia stared into the jocular face of a plump lady helper. 'No, I don't.' Lydia sat down immediately.

Worse was to follow. A young comedienne dressed up as an ancient Cockney was intent on leading the group in community singing. Lydia had never felt so damned insulted in her life. She clenched her jaws tightly shut. Benny, aware of her anger, kept gently gripping her hand. The songs lashed into Lydia as the company gave in to the exhortations of the helpers and joined in. The repertoire ended with a gleeful number called 'I'm One of the Ruins that Cromwell Knocked About a Bit'. This did finish Lydia off. As the applause broke, she got up from her seat and marched swiftly towards the exit. Benny kept close behind her.

Her way out was barred by two more smiling ladies. 'You'll miss the Bingo, dear. There are over fifteen prizes, and no end of boobies. It'll be a laugh. You shouldn't miss it. You never know, you might win a hamper or two tickets to the Palladium.'

Lydia would not have stayed if she had been offered a ticket to Heaven. Come to think of it, that's what the afternoon had felt like and she was not ready for Heaven yet. Lydia gently detached the restraining hand from her own.

'No, thank you. I really must go. I have an appointment,' she said.

'Oh, it can't be that important.' The woman was most insistent.

'It's with the doctor,' said Lydia.

'Oh, oh, I'm sorry. Nothing serious?' the woman asked.

'No, I'm pregnant,' said Lydia, leaving the astonished woman gasping after her as she and Benny strode out arm in arm into the cold, bright, winter's day.

A frost had formed on the pavement. The sky was blue, no hint of snow, but the early afternoon had prematurely covered the streets with a pretty but treacherous white film. They held on to each other firmly, and picked their way carefully along. One of them could not slip or fall without the other. They did not discuss this peril which was all about them, although both were conscious of it.

'You're not, are you? You're not pregnant?' he asked.

'Of course not. I ought to be if things were fair. I have enough of you inside of me. I feel pregnant, not sick in the morning or anything like that – but I feel as I always wanted to feel when I actually was pregnant. On both occasions when I told Henry I was having a baby all he did was work out the cost. He didn't kiss me or leap up with joy like fathers do in films. He just worked out a budget and cancelled our holiday in Bognor. Each time, he said we couldn't afford it. It was as though I had done something wrong. I think he found it distasteful. Towards the end, in the last month or so, when I got really big, he insisted on doing the shopping. Said it wasn't good for me to carry things, so that I hardly ever left the house. I'd just walk around and around the garden. I don't think he wanted people to see me like that – swollen with his child.

'Once, when I could feel our first baby moving inside of me, I told him, "Place your hand on my stomach," I said, "and you can feel it." "Never talk like that again, Lydia," he said, so I never did. Both my babies were secrets that I was not allowed to share. Now that they are grown up, they don't feel part of me at all. The more I see of them, the less impressed I am. It is as though I'd never had a family. Am I unnatural?'

'You're the most natural woman I've ever known,' Benny answered.

'Have you known many? I mean, have you known many like you know me?'

'Three or four.' He stopped and turned towards her. 'No, fifteen or twenty. Most of them before I was married – but I did have two on the side when I was married. That's the truth,' he said.

Lydia was not tempted to ask about the women, 'What were they like?' 'How had he met them?' She was not retrospectively jealous or even curious. So Benny had deceived his former wife twice, but this was nothing in comparison with the way Henry had deceived her. There were worse forms of deception than adultery – yet people tended to make such a fuss about it. Perhaps Henry had taken something on the side himself when he had deserted her bed. She found this thought consoling rather than hurtful.

Benny stopped to buy a mid-day *Evening News*. He turned to the centre pages and studied the racing meetings very carefully. Lydia shuddered. It was cold standing about but she made no visible remonstration. She enjoyed watching the races on Saturday afternoon. Benny had introduced her to it gradually and it had reached a point where she shared his enthusiasm. Indeed, it had gone one point or two further in that she now shared a bet with him. Not a lot of money, just 55p each, and for this they watched four of the races avidly. Benny had explained the bet which was called a 'Yankee'. Lydia had never quite understood it, but if all four horses won (which they never had), she and Benny would inherit so many cross doubles, so many trebles and an accumulator. Benny chose two horses because of their past form and Lydia chose two horses that had attractive-sounding names. Only once had the combination of study and aesthetics been successful and they had won £3.25 each when two of their horses had won. Both were Benny's choices. Benny placed two ticks by the two names and passed the paper to Lydia.

'Choose your two and I'll go and place the bet. Here's the key, love. Let yourself in and I'll be back in a jiffy. You're getting cold standing here.' His benevolence and concern always impressed her.

'There,' said Lydia, marking the paper after a swift glance. 'I'll back these two – "Take a Chance" and "Just a Stroll", nice names for horses.'

Benny frowned as he glanced at her selections. 'They're both outsiders. One has never run before and the other one fell on his last two outings.'

'Oh, dear, shall I change them?' Lydia asked.

'No, no, they've got four legs like all the other horses. Stick to your bet.' He always said that and Lydia never felt uncomfortable about watching her horses gallop along to finish at the rear of the field. The bet was just entertainment value as far as she was concerned. Benny had left her and she returned to his home. She lit the gas fire and turned on the TV. She giggled to herself – her horses might have four legs, but for that matter so had the kitchen table, and that wasn't going to win a race.

Benny arrived back just as the last of the television adverts were over. Lydia had poured out two glasses of sherry. This had become a routine which was both relaxing and enjoyable.

'I'm just in time, then. One of your horses is in the first race, the other in the last. Mine come in between.' He settled himself beside Lydia, and the two of them watched the horses being paraded in the paddock. 'Twenty-two runners, a large field, three-mile race with no end of jumps. It's going to be like the charge of the bloody Light Brigade. If you can find a winner amongst this lot, you can find anything,' he said, as he took a sip of sherry, and laughed. Lydia joined him. The horses were being assembled for what appeared to be a very ragged start.

'It's very pretty, isn't it? That's my horse. It's very small compared with the others. Green and white hoops my jockey is wearing. Green is supposed to be an unlucky colour,' said Lydia, giving up all hope before the race had begun.

'They oughtn't to be racing, really. The sun has melted the frost and I don't think it's really fair to jump them,' said Benny compassionately. The flag, in spite of Benny's conjectures, was held aloft. The horses were off.

'Good Lord,' said Lydia, as she watched her horse sprint ahead of the field whilst the other horses seemed to dawdle.

'"Take a Chance" has now sprinted into an early lead of some ten lengths or more.' The commentator's voice did not convey any enthusiasm at this initial outburst from Lydia's horse, which she thought looked more like a pony.

Benny poured more cold water on the commentator's statement by adding, 'It's a long course, inexperienced jockey, the horse will run out of steam. You can't start a three-mile hurdle like that. They have a long way to go yet. They have to go round the course twice and keep on their feet.'

'At least he's trying,' said Lydia, who watched her tiny horse leap the third hurdle neatly and politely.

' "Take a Chance" is now some fifteen clear lengths ahead
of the rest of the field, but there is still a long way to go. The
rest are fairly closely bunched, almost certainly biding their
time to make a challenge around the second circuit. Yes, the
rest of the field are maintaining a sensible pace.' Lydia felt
that the commentator was not being fair. Her little horse
was jumping its heart out. She edged forward on her chair.
She murmured quiet encouragement to the horse and rider.

'Don't look behind. You just keep going!'

Some two or three minutes later she had gone quite
silent. The horses had rounded the final bend and were in
the home straight. The commentator was still cynical about
Lydia's chances. 'Three more fences to jump and "Take
Your Chance" is now being caught by the field, only four
lengths clear and, oh, oh, what a mess! There's a pile-up.
Three, perhaps four, horses are down. It doesn't look as
though anyone is injured. The field is spread-eagled now.
"Take Your Chance" has only to jump the last fence for an
easy win.'

She watched her horse cross the line and then saw a
close-up of the animal in the unsaddling enclosure. Steam
rose from its back and white foam from its jaws. The jockey
took its saddle off and a trainer threw a blanket over the
sweating horse. The jockey patted its neck. Her horse's
name and a number flashed across the screen.

'Dear God,' said Benny. 'It's 33–1; it's a 33–1 winner!'

'I knew he wouldn't fall,' said Lydia adamantly.

After the third race, Lydia was most concerned. Both of
Benny's horses had passed the winning-post before any of
the others. Benny could not keep still. He sat up, stood up,
sat down and paced about the room.

'We've a 33-to-1 winner, a 7-to-2 winner, and a 4-to-1
winner. If your last horse comes in, we've got a little
fortune. There's no price quoted for your last horse. What's
its name again?' His agitation worried her.

' "Just a Stroll".' She tried to sound as complacent about it
as possible. The advertisements before the next race, and
the last, seemed interminable – yet another one on cold
cures. At last the screen returned them to the race course.

'It's over the sticks again. Mine were on the flat.' Benny

fiddled with the set so that the sound was much too loud. He did not seem to be aware of the booming voice of the presenter. He began to pace about the room. Lydia felt she should be assertive. This couldn't be good for his heart. She got up from her seat and turned the volume of the set down. She stood there with her hand on the knob.

'Benny, sit down, sit down on the settee. If you don't, I'll turn it off. Sit down on the settee. I'll join you. We'll sit together and we'll sit still.' Benny acknowledged that her order was based on good sense. There would be no point in winning if you couldn't enjoy it. His breath had already begun to come in quick jerks. She glared at him. 'Sit on the settee!' she commanded. He obeyed quietly. She sat next to him and took his arm, and they watched and waited. Neither spoke until the race was over.

'What does all that mean?' Lydia asked.

'It means we'll have to wait longer for the result. It's a photo-finish and there is also a stewards' inquiry. Although the inquiry won't affect our horse. He wasn't involved in the bumping,' he murmured. He seemed exhausted. Lydia was not hopeful of a successful outcome. It did look as though their horse had been beaten. She relayed her thoughts to Benny.

'The angle's deceptive,' he answered her quickly. Benny was an optimist.

The result was announced. 'Just a Stroll', their horse, had won by a nose.

'Won by a nose!' Lydia exclaimed.

'We've won a small fortune,' said Benny, and kissed her neck.

'Won by a nose! How long is a horse's nose?' asked Lydia.

'About an inch and a half,' said Benny.

'Good Lord, imagine it, us winning all this money by a horse's nose. Poor thing, it must have been straining its head forward.'

'It's over a thousand,' said Benny.

'Pardon?'

'We've won over £1,000. Are you coming with me to collect?'

'I think I'd better,' said Lydia. Then she restrained him from rising from the settee. 'We'll have another sherry before we go. Let's just calm down a bit.' They did. Then they collected their money as calmly as they did when they were given their pensions at the post office.

7

'Dear ——,
I have booked myself into a hotel for Christmas and the New Year. I hope you don't mind. It's all to do with a section of the 'Know Your City' class.

I am enclosing a cheque for £20 and you may all choose your presents from it. It seems the most sensible thing to do as presents are always a disappointment once you've taken the wrapping off. Have a Happy Christmas and a Festive New Year.

Love to you all,
Lydia.'

The identical cards to Hertfordshire and Surrey were written quickly, with no pause – except for signature. Lydia had almost written 'Mother', and then, for some reason not quite known to her, she had changed her mind.

'We've just kept to traditional English foliage for decoration. All those paper stretchers and shiny tinsel look so common. They make a home look more like a shop window. They've nothing, nothing to do with a real Christmas.' Eileen placed a trail of holly sprigs along the mantelshelf. Barbara murmured agreement with Eileen's sentiments without really considering them. Paula felt there was something odd about the decoration: not the idea, but there was something . . . Paula smiled with sudden insight. The holly was barren. There was not a berry to be seen. Aunty Eileen's clever meanness had not escaped her. Aunty Eileen and Uncle Derek had just trimmed their hedge at the bottom of the garden. Some of the holly leaves were a mottled green. These, too, were barren. Paula thought she might mention the berries but decided not to be spiteful.

'Holly is very expensive, Aunty.' Paula spoke with a sweet, false generosity that her aunt did not detect.

'Yes, it is, dear, but Christmas is only once a year. Sometimes expense shouldn't come in to things.' Eileen held out a spray of prickle to Paula – 'Could you just balance that along the top of the picture, dear? The one of the wild elephant in the gold frame. It will look nice against the frame.'

Paula took it from her aunt. 'Silly bitch', she thought, and took the maximum amount of time in placing the artistic sprig in its allocated place above the elephant.

Barbara made no attempt to join in her sister-in-law's pre-Christmas Eve preparations. She leafed through the coffee-table book on wild flowers, flipping the pages over noisily. Odd words like 'harebell' and 'stinkwort' caught her eye. She made no effort to look at the illustrations. It was her way of sulking. A few moments earlier Eileen had suggested that Lydia had been somewhat unfair in sending £20 to each family. 'After all, dear, there are four of us, and my children are still growing. Still, I don't suppose Mother had thought about it; as we've all agreed, she is getting a bit forgetful – but I'm sure she would have meant us to share the money equally. Of course, it's not something I'd like to discuss with her. She always gets so upset when she realizes she has been thoughtless.'

'We'll pool the £40 and share it between the seven of us,' Barbara conceded without argument. They were Derek's and Eileen's guests for three days. No point in beginning the family arrangement with a quarrel. But Barbara decided to eat like an ox and make up for the loss. She could always diet later.

Her husband had joined her brother. The 'boys' had gone to fly kites on Box Hill. Paula had been invited and shocked Eileen by saying out loud, in front of the children, that she was suffering from period pains, thus excusing herself from getting bored and cold without an inane discussion.

'I ordered a large capon from my butcher. He's so good, he says capon is much more tasty than turkey. I believe it's a cross between chicken and turkey. It gives the best of both birds – size from the turkey and succulence from the chicken,' Eileen chirped brightly.

'It's nothing of the kind. If your butcher told you that, he is a liar,' said Paula. Barbara kept silent – let Paula punish. Eileen deserved it. If Eileen had not mentioned the money, she might have silenced her daughter.

Eileen turned abruptly from the mantelshelf and clenched a piece of holly in her rage. 'Ouch, ooh, now, look what you've made me do.' She sucked her finger. 'Paula, I do not need lessons in culinary advice from you. If you have never tasted capon, how could you possibly be so . . .'

'I was speaking biologically,' said Paula, picking up the piece of holly that her aunt had dropped on the floor. 'A capon, Aunty Eileen, a capon is a castrated cockerel.' She handed the holly back to her aunt.

'I'm going to the kitchen to prepare the stuffing,' Eileen muttered and left the room almost in tears.

'Now, you've upset your aunt,' said Barbara.

'Yes, I know,' said Paula, without a trace of regret.

'Your history result has surprised me. I never dreamed you would do so well. You must have worked very hard, darling.' Barbara had decided to be nice to her daughter. She closed the flower book and waited for a response.

'I didn't work very hard. I didn't have to. My tutor gave me some extra time. I go over to see him of an evening, usually once a week.'

'How old is he?'

'About thirty. It's difficult to tell. Sometimes he looks younger.'

'Do you go there alone?'

'Yes.'

'Er . . . his wife and family must be very forbearing. You oughtn't to make too many demands, Paula. Teachers have a life of their own, you know.' Barbara used her professional tone.

'He's not married.'

'What? How long do you stay? What time do you leave?'

'Usually around 11 p.m., then Stephen collects me. The tutor invites me. I don't demand. He likes me. He thinks I'm original.' Paula watched her mother squirm in discomfort before crossing her legs. Paula intervened before the cautioning, rational lecture could begin. 'Don't worry, he's not interested in that. He's camp. He lives with his friend.'

Barbara swallowed hard and got up from her seat. 'I'll give Aunty Eileen a hand with the onions,' she said.

Paula was glad to be left alone. She felt fretful. And, like all the other members of the family, she was feeling cross about Gran's card. If Gran had divulged her plans, Stephen might not have left for Wolverhampton so soon after the term had finished. They might have had a couple of days together at Gran's house and parted company embracing one another. As it was, they had parted with a quarrel and he had walked away from her, giving her the last word.

'You are insignificant,' she had said to him.

He had refused to join the Students 'Action Group' without giving her a reason, and she had become angry. How could he maintain so much lethargy when there was so much to care about?

'I care about you,' he had said.

Paula reflected on her answer. She lit a cigarette. She whispered the phrase 'You are insignificant.' She puffed at her cigarette and began to weep. 'I didn't mean it. I didn't mean it.'

She spoke out aloud to the holly and the elephant but they could not offer her any comfort.

She did not hear her two young, male cousins enter the lounge. They had been trained to remove their shoes before stepping on the fitted carpet. Nevertheless, she was grateful for their existence. The boys made no attempt at greeting or conversation. All three had long since truthfully acknowledged that they disliked one another, so they were as economical as possible about what they shared. The television was switched on. The boys sat cross-legged on the floor, totally obstructing Paula's view. She picked up the book on flowers and studied the illustrations without reading the words. Her Uncle Derek, who always made strenuous efforts to engage Paula in conversation, put an end to her retreat. As usual, he was jolly, enthusiastic and familiar. He came in and placed an arm about her shoulder. He often did this. He would have liked to place it elsewhere but he refused to admit this to himself. Paula did not move when he touched her.

'And how is our lady professor today? Not still studying, I hope. You should have come with us. A breath of fresh air would have done you good.'

Paula leaned forward, placed the book on the table and reached for a cigarette. He removed his arm.

'Those aren't going to do your lungs any good,' he said.

'How were the kites?' she asked him.

'Well, they went up in the air. We had great fun, didn't we, lads?'

The boys nodded. Derek tried a little harder.

'What do you expect kites to do, then?' he grinned at her.

'Not all of them get up in the air. Some get entangled in trees and when I've run with one it's always nose-dived into the ground. I would say they are more prone to accidents than most things.'

'We did lose one, in fact. The tailings snapped and it spun round and round.' He gestured with his hand.

'I'm sorry,' said Paula.

'Oh, we can always make another. It's all part of the fun.'

'What, losing them?

'Yes, yes, I suppose so. It's not something to get serious about.' He often accused Paula of being serious. Perhaps it wasn't right to think too much. As far as he was concerned, if you thought, you couldn't be happy or funny.

'Did you skate as a child, Uncle Derek?' she asked him.

'Why, no. Whatever made you think of that?'

'Oh, I don't know, but I can picture you skimming around, spinning from one place to another. Gliding here and there and . . .' The rest of the adults joined them.

Eileen was in better humour. Barbara had made amends by helping in the kitchen. The adults all chose to drink gin and tonic; the boys were offered and accepted lemonade.

'Would you like a glass of cider or a shandy, Paula?' Eileen placed a chronological category on drinks.

'Gin, please, with just a little tonic.' Eileen frowned and gave Paula a drink which consisted of tonic water with the mildest dash of gin.

'It's really not like Mother, to just send a card like this at such short notice. I would have thought she would have enjoyed a family Christmas.' Derek spoke to his sister but his wife continued with the subject.

'She might have given us all a little more notice. Her arrangements must have been very sudden. I bought some sherry for her; I know she enjoys the occasional glass. I suppose she forgets the budgeting side of hospitality.' Eileen sipped her drink.

'It's very strange,' said Barbara.

'That she hasn't left us an address. We don't even know where she has gone.'

'You're right. It's a bit insensitive. Anything might happen to her and we wouldn't know where she was,' said Eric.

'She's not going to die, Daddy. Could I have a little more gin in this, please?' Paula crossed the room and handed her glass to Eileen.

'I agree with Eric. We ought to know where she is.' Eileen did not let Paula take the gin bottle from her hand.

'We could telephone Mr Burford, get his number from the directory. His family will surely know where the group are based.' They all agreed that Barbara's suggestion was sensible, and with due family concern they found his telephone number.

Eric dialled the number.

'This is Mr Burford, yes, Bunty. Is that you, Michael, *mon cher*?'

'No, it's not. My name is Eric Reading. I'm telephoning on behalf of my mother-in-law, Lydia Poulton. I believe she attends your classes.'

'Yes, she is a darling.'

Eric put his hand over the mouthpiece and whispered to the company, 'The man sounds peculiar, drunk, I think.' He removed his hand from the mouthpiece. Barbara waved her hand with an impatient gesture, anxious to hear more news rather than her husband's interpretation of what sort of body or person hung at the other end of a telephone line.

'Ahem, I do think it is an excellent idea – that is, the idea that the elderly can group themselves, away from home and have a holiday at Christmas time. Although I do think the project is a bit divisive as far as we are concerned. It's not as though our mother is alone. She has a family and we would have liked her with us.' Approving nods from the adults in the lounge greeted Eric's remarks.

'I'm sorry, ducks, I don't know what you're talking about,' came Bunty's reply. He had, in fact, been drinking since eleven that morning. 'Is this a hoax, because if it is, Merry Christmas, tra-la-la and goodbye!' he added.

'Wait, wait,' Eric called, nervously, down the mouthpiece. He continued more quietly when he realized that Bunty had not replaced the receiver. 'We have to approach this matter calmly. I have already explained who I am.'

'Yes, dear. Just stop fart-arsing around and come to the point,' Bunty hiccupped.

'I do not like your tone, Mr Burford,' said Eric, curtly.

'Oh, please don't start quarrelling, Eric.' Barbara jumped up in exasperation and got her new perm entangled in some holly.

'I was born with it, born with it, dear. Now what in hell do you want?' Bunty was getting angry.

'My mother-in-law, Mrs Lydia Poulton, has informed us by card that she is staying over Christmas and the New Year in a hotel with a section of the "Know Your London" class of whom you are the tutor. Unfortunately, she has failed to give us the address of the whereabouts of the hotel. You know how the elderly can be forgetful. Presumably, as the course tutor responsible for these – these – er, arrangements, you could kindly give us her address. Naturally, as her kith and kin, we are a little concerned.' Eric was at his pedantic best, and Eileen smiled approval. She did wish Derek could talk like Eric at times.

'It's nothing to do with me, dear. It must be a private arrangement Lydia has made,' Bunty tittered.

'What?' Eric snapped into the telephone.

'A private arrangement is what I said, and one more thing, darling: your mother-in-law is never forgetful. Goodbye – Happy Christmas.'

Eric listened to the burring sound from the receiver and stood quite speechless still holding on to the telephone as if it were electrified. 'He said that Mother's arrangements were private. They are not connected with the class. She's told us a pack of lies.' He placed the receiver down.

Eileen helped herself to a large glass of sherry. Tears trickled down her cheeks.

'After all the trouble I've taken, this is all the thanks I get. It's plain deceit, that's what it is. Deceit.' She sat down and was duly comforted by her husband. 'Unless, unless, of course, her mind has begun to wander. It does happen at a certain age. I was reading a book about it the other day. It can happen quite suddenly. One minute an elderly person can be quite sane and then,' Eileen snapped her fingers, 'then just *non compos mentis.*' She shook her head sadly.

Eric gave a pedagogic frown. 'Do you think we should contact the police? If she is wandering around willy-nilly, anything might happen and . . .'

'That won't be necessary.' Paula, who had remained silent, could not listen to the clap-trap any long. She lit a cigarette, inhaled deeply, let them wait until she was ready, making the most of this moment of control. 'She hasn't told lies. She has gone with a section of the group. Well, one section of it.' She laughed somewhat bitterly.

'Paula?' Barbara's voice had become quite faint.

'She's gone away with a man. He attends the class. He's a retired ironmonger. She's having it off with him.'

'What do you mean?' asked Derek, putting his arm about his wife who had now begun to sob.

'In genteel terms, Uncle, she is having an affair. She is sleeping with the man. They fuck together.'

'Paula!'

'Oh, I must go to the bathroom. I'm going to be sick,' wailed Eileen. Derek helped her in her state of semi-collapse from the room.

'We must see Mother when she returns. We must see her as a family,' said Barbara disapprovingly.

Barbara and Eric left to join Eileen. This present situation demanded a unified but dignified opposition. The situation had to be approached and destroyed sensibly.

Paula was left to herself in the lounge. Funny, no one had noticed the two boys, whose eyes were still fixed on the television.

'I've done it,' she thought. 'First with Stephen and now with Gran.' In her desolation and anger she seized a cushion and threw it at the elephant picture, knocking it askew. Before she could make any self-analysis about the reasons for her spitefulness, there was a call for dinner. Family recovery was swift in the face of adversity.

In spite of the dreadful and shocking information they had received, the family tucked into the meal with gusto. Eileen was showered with compliments by her guests, and this flattery induced an amazing steel-like recovery from her former state of hysteria. Only Paula picked and prodded at her food. She managed to swallow only a few mouthfuls of the vegetables. While the others gorged, she moved bits of food about her plate, making a space here or a space there but eating little. She had no appetite.

'You haven't touched your capon, dear, and I've given you a wing,' observed Eileen as she removed a small bone from her mouth and returned it to the side of her plate.

'I think I'm going vegetarian,' said Paula.

The truth was that she was afraid to stab the dead cockerel with her fork even if the bird had been castrated. She was not religious but it had entered her mind that if she prodded the cooked fowl with her fork it might crow three times. Such was the extent and depth of her sense of betrayal.

8

Lydia drew the collar of her simulated fur coat up above the back of her head and held the large lapels over her ears to keep out the cold. The coat had been Benny's idea. It was fawn and white in colour. It would show the dirt quickly but Lydia relished the thought that her choice of a garment did not have to be sensible. At the moment, it felt so good and it must have looked good as Benny always stroked her a lot when she wore it. His hand was, at this moment, resting on her behind. They surveyed the orange-coloured car which stood outside Benny's house.

'I've hired it for a fortnight,' he said.

'Benny, I know it's silly of me but I hadn't imagined that you could drive,' said Lydia, as Benny unlocked the door to the front seat of the car and settled her in position. He did not answer until he was sitting beside her and had placed the ignition key in place.

'I drove an ambulance during the war. I've kept my licence ever since.' He started the engine, and the car moved. He turned the corner into the main road. 'The doctor advised me not to drive after my first attack. He didn't say that I should never drive. He just advised me not to. I'm a risk, Lydia, do you understand? You're taking a risk travelling with me. I'll stop the car, now, if you want me to.'

Lydia had placed a hand on his knee. She did not feel any concern. On the contrary, his information elated her.

'Drive on, Benny, drive on. We are at risk all the time, both of us. How much nicer to be at risk together. Just look for the danger signs of the road. Ignore our own. We don't have time to dwell on them.'

'Where are we making for first, then?' he asked.

'We are spending the night in the New Forest at a hotel which was an old manor house. I've worked out the route.

It should take us about three hours. We leave for Lyme Regis the following morning. I have it all planned, all booked.'

'Clever girl,' he said, and placed his foot more firmly on the accelerator.

Lazenby Manor looked as it did in the photograph in the brochure Lydia had obtained. The building came into view as the car entered the long, tree-lined private drive. Both Lydia and Benny had ceased commenting on the wild ponies as there were so many of them cropping what fodder they could from the road side. Lovely animals, Lydia had marvelled, at her first glance of them, and Benny could not quite believe in their existence until he had seen several of them. 'They look like Apache ponies,' he had said. He said it would be a pity to ride them – even a Red Indian on one of their backs wouldn't have looked right. It was as though the ponies owned the place. The human visitors were the intruders, yet the creatures seemed to bear them no malice; indeed, they appeared curiously indifferent to humanity.

So were the reception committee at the hotel. The flower arrangements in the vestibule were impressive, not a plastic bloom in sight. Chrysanthemums and holly were arranged most tastefully, leaping from urns and what seemed to be enormous antique vases of great value. A forlorn-looking stag's head protruded from one of the walls, and a huge shield bearing a coat of arms hung above the archway that stretched across the wide, winding staircase. A suit of armour (like the ones Lydia had seen at the Tower of London) stood at the foot of the stairway. One metal hand rested on the wooden banister. You could smell the polish. The woodwork shone. Small settees and window-seats decorated the vestibule, although no one seemed to dare to sit on them. However, the presence of these *objets d'art* enhanced the air of a country manor house which the hotel management sought to exude. As she and Benny approached the reception cubicle, Lydia felt a bit like an interloper, as if she were an uninvited guest who had perchance dropped in on the landed gentry. Lydia and Benny stood side by side at the desk together.

'Ah, is it Mr and Mrs Poulton? It's just for tonight, isn't it?' The receptionist seemed to be in a great hurry and hardly glanced at her guests, who had no time to answer either of her questions. She put two crosses in a large book which lay open on the desk before her. 'Dinner is between 7 and 10 p.m., breakfast between 7.30 and 9.30 a.m. Your room number is 611. Here is your key. Have you parked your car near the laurel bushes? Good.'

Lydia was rather taken aback by some of the information. Could there possibly be so many rooms in the hotel? It certainly didn't look that large – perhaps there were turrets at the back. She hoped Benny didn't mind being called Mr Poulton. She was sure she had given his correct name when she had confirmed the booking. Benny seemed unaffected by the receptionist's sweet, cold efficiency. He took the key from the desk.

'We'd like some tea now if you can manage it. We've been travelling for some time. Is it possible to have it brought to our room?'

'Tea and coffee are available in every room, sir. You will find all you need there – kettle, cups and saucers, tea pots, coffee, tea, sugar. If you took note of the brochure, you will see that each room is also provided with a colour television set for extra comfort. We try to do our very best for our guests. Your comfort is our pleasure.'

Lydia thought she sounded a bit like the lady on that telephone where you dialled the time.

'Thank you,' said Benny. He and Lydia turned to negotiate the impressive staircase.

'Excuse me, excuse me.' They were called back to the desk. 'I'm sorry, I should have given you instructions as to the geography of the hotel,' said the receptionist. 'You are in Nightingale Wing. Go straight down the corridor on your left, then turn right at the end of it. You will come to another corridor with blue and white doors. You can't miss it. Walk to the end of that corridor and you will arrive at the back entrance of the hotel. Cross the gravel pathway and you will see three buildings. They are all marked. One is Curie, one is Cavell, the other, your one, is Nightingale. I believe that your room is on the second floor. There is a self-operating lift service. I'm sure everything will be to your liking.'

Lydia held out no such hope. It sounded more like a hospital than a hotel.

A little bewildered by the rapid delivery of their room's whereabouts, Lydia raised her hand to her brow. She was confused as to precisely where to go and felt foolish. Much to her relief, Benny had already begun to move. She smiled. She admired Benny's unfussy practicality. Clearly he had noted the details firmly in his head. She followed on behind him along the corridors. They did not have to pause for questions. They reached the back entrance of the hotel without any problems. Lydia breathed deep snatches of night air. It was good to be independent. The gravel pathway lay in front of them, and some twenty yards beyond stood the tower blocks.

'It looks like a council estate,' said Lydia, feeling somewhat cheated. She took the case from Benny, who had grunted an assent to her remark.

'I'll carry it for the rest of the time,' she said.

He accepted her offer and eventually pressed the lift button for the second floor. Room 611 emphasized the modernity of the tower blocks which they had arrived at in their flight from London into the New Forest. Lydia had imagined a large bedroom with a huge double bed covered with a floral canopy. Perhaps even a chamber pot. She had expected to be housed in a manor house – like the ones she had read about in romantic novels. Instead, she stepped into what to all intents and purposes was a small, comfortable, modern flat. She couldn't really complain about the comforts of the place. A separate bathroom and toilet were encased within it. It had two lovely brand-new armchairs. There were side lamps, a coffee table and a writing desk. The colour television was attached to the wall with a chain and stood in the left-hand corner of the room. A small hatch held the kettle with tea, coffee, milk and cream, all labelled in sachets. However, she could not suppress the sigh of dismay as she glanced at the sleeping arrangements.

'What's wrong, love? Are you a bit tired?' Benny had heard the sigh.

'Single beds. I hate single beds. I'm sorry. I have an aversion to them,' said Lydia.

'Pull the covers off them. Push them together and we can make the two beds up as a double one.'

'Oh, dear, do you think they'll mind?'

'We're paying for our stay here. It's none of their business how we sleep. Anyway, we're so far away, who is to know?'

'Yes, it is very private here,' Lydia added. Benny had already pushed the beds together. Lydia removed the sheets and blankets and followed his suggestions accordingly. As if to make amends for her declared disappointment, she looked out from the window. 'We have a balcony. You can see the trees. It's a lovely view,' she said.

'I'll put the kettle on,' said Benny.

Twenty minutes later, they were sipping tea in bed, feeling warm, relaxed and private. It was about 7 p.m. Someone had left a book behind. It was called *Gideon's Bible*. On examining it Lydia found that, apart from its title, the content seemed identical to most other Bibles. She placed it carefully underneath her side of the bed, so that if the owner returned she would know where to find it quickly.

Their mindful but enjoyable silence was broken by a scraping and bumping sound which must have come from the next room.

'The walls must be very thin,' observed Lydia.

'Sounds as though they're doing what we did. Just rearranging things a bit,' Benny chuckled.

'My husband didn't like me to touch him.' Lydia had placed her hand casually between Benny's thighs. He responded by stroking her belly. Neither of them was aroused in any way. The physical actions denoted a trusting proximity rather than sensuous movement or sexuality. This was often the case when they caressed.

'Once or twice I did try to hold him, touch him. I felt I needed to. You see, it was difficult to talk to him except about details of the house or expenditure. He was a very thrifty man. Gradually, I came to the conclusion that he thought I was stupid. I felt that if I couldn't talk I could let him know what I felt in other ways. He rejected them, and for the latter years of our marriage I had no love for him. Well, I did, but he just wouldn't allow it. He became a lodger I was fond of. I did get a part-time job as a helper in a school – I was so lonely. After three days, he found out about the job and put a stop to it. He said there was no need for me to work. He said he wanted me at home. It would have been easier to accept if I had felt I was a bit more than a housekeeper. Yes, that's what I was, a married house-keeper. He said that if I worked, it would affect his income tax. I didn't quarrel about it. The children supported him. I've never had anyone I could talk to about these things . . .'

Lydia's reminiscences were interrupted by a knocking noise. She withdrew her hand from Benny's groin. 'I think there's someone at the door. You'd better put your dressing-gown on, Benny.'

Benny placed one leg out of bed, then paused. There was something strange about the knocking. It was almost rhyth-mic. Lydia was a little surprised when after a few minutes Benny got back under the sheets again without leaving the bed side. The knocking persisted.

'Benny, I can hear . . .'

'It's not the door, love. The noise is coming from the next room,' he interrupted Lydia.

He looked at Lydia and smiled. Benny smiled slowly. Lydia loved his smile. It increased the wrinkles about his mouth and eyes and gave his face an impish quality. The knocking grew louder and then Lydia heard a woman's gasp. It was then that she too smiled. In fact, she began to giggle. Benny found her laughter infectious and they were forced gently to subdue each other's mirth. When the giggling had stopped, they listened intently to the gasps and bumps which came from the room beyond. Lydia was not sure whether this inadvertent erotic exercise had been the cause, but Benny's member had grown and hardened in her hand. She did not draw away, for a strange excitement had also possessed her.

Benny had begun to kiss her – everywhere. Cunilingus always sent her into raptures but the noise from the other room aroused her further and increased her sexual sense of adventure. She wanted to please Benny too; it took no great effort for her to swivel about in the bed. She caressed his member and took it in her mouth. She heard his grunt of pleasure and felt his tongue about inside of her. How long they continued in this fashion Lydia did not know. However, she experienced more orgasms than ever before in her life. During one such tremor Benny spilled himself into the back of her throat. Lydia gulped and lay back exhausted. The love-making noises from next door had ceased. The room was oddly silent. The double-glazed windows excluded noise from the outside.

'We must have beaten them on the straight,' said Benny as Lydia returned to her original position with her head next to his.

'I've never done that before.' Lydia spoke without a trace of shame.

'You were marvellous. I could eat you. Christ, I'm lucky to have found you.' He hugged her in his huge arms. She lay with her head in his armpit. She liked his smell. Both were soon snoring, a natural outcome of mutual satisfaction.

Lydia yawned and wallowed in her state of torpor and drowsiness, only half awake. She attempted to snuggle closer to Benny. He was not there. Abruptly she opened her eyes and sat bolt upright in a state of semi-wakeful panic. She was relieved to see his broad back, which was now enveloped in a navy blue woollen dressing gown. He was facing the kettle hatch, and she watched him place the cups and saucers on the table by its side. Even the spoons he put in position so that no sound was made. He padded across the carpet in his bare feet and collected a package she had wrapped herself. It contained sandwiches. They had not eaten all of them on the journey down. He saw her as he turned.

'I didn't want to wake you.' He unwrapped the package and arranged the sandwiches on a large plate on the table. Lydia looked for her watch and, as she picked it up, he spoke. 'It's half past ten, darlin'. We're too late for dinner, now. Still, we have enough to be going on with here.' He gestured towards the tea and sandwiches.

'There are some mince pies in the plastic box.' Funny mixture, thought Lydia. Sex, sleep and mince pies. She laughed. How much better it was to be eating egg and tomato sandwiches in their own room. Carols drifted from the radio. No table or group etiquettes impeded their communication. Benny was solicitous as only he could be, pouring her tea, patting her hand occasionally, even joining in with a snatch of a carol and singing to her. In the middle of the mince pies, the egg and tomato sandwiches, the tea and the carols, Lydia talked about her love for him. She had not timed this or chosen the setting as young lovers so often do. That's what was so good about the two of them. Neither contrived.

'I love you, Benny. I really do and I don't mind saying it.' She bit into a mince pie.

'I like to hear you say it. Do you want another cuppa?'

'Yes, please, not too much milk. No, I mean, I love you apart from the er . . .' She glanced at the rumpled bedclothes. He followed her gaze.

'Oh, yes, I know that. You and me are mates. You're my mate, as well as my . . .'

'Lover,' she said.

'Yes, and that's rare, my girl, rare, I tell you.'

They watched the late-night film on television. It was an old Ealing comedy film, full of caricatures rather than characters. They held hands and chuckled. Some of the players were long since dead, and here they were, performing. Lydia felt chastened by the thought as she watched a funny old lady with three chins pedal furiously on a bicycle. All that was left of her now was this celluloid fragment.

'Each day is important to us, isn't it, Benny?' she asked him.

'Of course, it is, darlin'.' Fortunately Benny had not understood the full importance of Lydia's words.

'You're rare, rare and precious. You're my jewels,' said Lydia.

'You talk lovely,' he added, and they continued to watch the film. Sharing between them required no effort. Bliss was so easily achieved. It was good to be elderly and in love.

9

'Dear —————,

I should have written earlier, but the days have been so full that I just haven't got around to it sooner. I've started to write once or twice before and then something has cropped up and I've had to abandon the letter. I will probably be back in London by the time this reaches you, but at least you will know that I did think of you all.

Lyme Regis is so different from Bognor Regis. With both towns having 'Regis' written after them I thought that they might be similar but they're not: no, they are not one bit alike. As you can see, Lyme Regis is in Dorset, only just, as Devon is only a mile or two away. The weather has been cold but dry, so we have wrapped up well and done quite a lot of walking. It's funny, but my leg has not troubled me at all and I haven't bothered to rest it as I usually do. In fact, I think the veins have gone down or gone back. Perhaps the tides here have affected them.

It's a very old town, and there are things on the shore line that are thousands of years old. They're called fossils; I've collected a few. The creatures have left their imprint on stone. Some are intricate and most beautiful – it's hard to believe that they were here such a long time ago. They are such a comfort to us as they make us feel timeless. Although I certainly don't feel like an old fossil. But, now, if anyone calls me an old fossil, I won't mind too much as they are so pretty. I have one which Paula will especially appreciate.

The sea-front is lovely to walk along and we have got used to the wind. The front twists round into a kind of elbow. The elbow part is called the Cobb. The Cobb is very old and there are wooden houses on it painted black. If we walk along, it's just like being in the time of Charles Dickens. Stuck in the sand near the Cobb are some jagged pieces of wood. They are known locally as Granny's Teeth. Rather cruel to call them by such a name. Anyway, they're much too big to belong to any grandmother.

Yesterday, we saw a fox – I mean, a real one – in a field. I'd never seen one before except in nature books. We had gone for a little drive. The surrounding countryside here is quite hilly, and we had turned down a very narrow lane – there was only room for one car. It was really more of a track than a lane so it was a good job there were no cars coming the other way. We parked the car near a small copse, just a few trees that seemed to have been dropped in the middle of a large field. We got out of the car, and there, not more than a hundred yards away from us, was the animal. It stared at us for a moment. I suppose it was as surprised as we were. Then it darted off. I'd thought that foxes slept through the winter but they don't. A farmer told us they will eat almost anything living – like beetles, worms and all sorts of crawling things. It must be hard for the foxes in the winter and I couldn't help but feel a bit sorry for the creature. Imagine what it must be like to be thinking where your next meal is coming from, day in and day out.

Sometimes, I wonder if we realize how lucky we are – I mean, half the things we worry about we shouldn't worry about at all. I would have liked to have taken a photograph of the fox but I forgot to bring my box camera with me. It's years since I felt the need to be using it. I've packed it away carefully somewhere, too carefully, and I just can't put my hand on it. Although, even if I had had the camera with me, I don't know that I would have had the presence of mind to take a snap-shot – we were much too astonished.

Well, it's another New Year. I must say I have never felt so well in all my life. It must be the sea air that has suited me. New Years are always exciting but we didn't get drunk or anything like that. However, we did 'see the year in' in a grand fashion.

I will telephone you all when I get home. I do hope that all your festivities were happy and pleasurable.

Love to you all,
Lydia.'

Eileen handed Lydia's letter to Barbara who had placed it on the table between them. Barbara had already scrutinized the letter's content. The daughter and daughter-in-law had found depths of affinity and kinship that they had not known existed until Lydia's duplicity and consequent erring adventure had come to light. They now met frequently and listened and confided to each other about the enormous pressures of family life that so often beset them both. They constantly sighed and shook their heads – but like the true heroines they had cast themselves as, they bore this tribulation with strength and fortitude.

'She must be home by now. She hasn't telephoned.' Eileen glared at the letter. Barbara's face looked puckered and saddened. She shook her head as if afflicted by Parkinson's disease.

'Do you think we should contact her?' Eileen asked.

'I think, I think we should look at the letter again. There's a lot about it gives me great cause for concern, Eileen dear,' said Barbara.

Eileen's face lit up with hope when Barbara used phrases like 'grave cause for concern'. It did not necessarily mean that Barbara was opting for a course of action that involved pity or compassion. On the contrary, it usually meant that some brutal, sensible solution was being hatched out. Eileen poured out two small glasses of sherry in anticipation of Barbara's plans or ideas. Not that she was celebrating anything; sherry was drunk at funerals too.

'I think Mother should see a doctor. I'm afraid for her health, as I know you must be, Eileen, darling.'

'You mean, the veins?' asked Eileen.

Barbara drew in her breath. Her sister-in-law's stupidity often irritated her. However, this was no time to show displeasure or debase Eileen's intellect – what there was of it.

'At times, Eileen, I think your kindness is your downfall. I mean, you have read this letter. You've read it carefully. Now, putting all kind thoughts aside, answer me truthfully. Do you consider this letter as the kind of letter our mother, as you know her, would write to us?' Barbara lowered her voice and gently held both of Eileen's hands in her own. 'Would you consider this a letter from a sane person?' she half whispered.

'Oh, oh, oh . . .' Eileen just managed to transform a satisfied smile into an expression of silent screen anguish.

Her histrionics would never have got her in front of the footlights of the very worst amateur dramatic society.

Barbara picked up the letter and held it gingerly by one corner, almost as though she did not wish to fingerprint a piece of vital evidence.

'If we get her committed, I suppose the two families will be executors of all property and any money that Mother has accumulated. Derek can go into that side of things. I'm sure we can settle it all amicably between us.' Eileen finished off her sherry.

Barbara replied before Eileen's empty glass had been put back on the table. 'Don't talk like that, Eileen. At least, not yet. Everything is in a premature state yet. Obviously, we have to get psychiatric and medical opinions on our side. For that, we need evidence, and this' – Barbara placed the letter on the table – 'this is our first piece of evidence. We must continue to glean, not put any restraints on Mother, and then, when we are sure, we must act. It seems a terrible thing to have to watch one's mother disintegrate before one can do anything about helping her, but that is the way things are nowadays. We have to work out all of this together, Eileen; keep notes, diaries of what she says and does. Compare and compile, until we have a sound case to present to the proper authorities. Then, as you correctly say, we can look into the materialistic aspects of the matter. Mother is by no means penniless. What she has now we wouldn't want her to squander away. As far as you and I are concerned, we know that Mother is mad. A cruel word, mad. However, we have to come to the assumption that she is either that – er, er, a or – er – a tart. She's not a tart, is she?'

'Oh, no, no,' said Eileen, generously.

The two women left the room arm in arm. Barbara had invited Eileen to select a plant from the greenhouse as a little going-away present. Eileen felt honoured as she had never been allowed to set foot in the greenhouse before. Paula watched them walk along the pathway from the kitchen window and then casually drifted into the empty lounge. Her mother and Aunt Eileen would never dream that she was bothered enough about anything to the point at which she might eavesdrop. But that is what she had done, with her ear gently placed outside the hall door. She had heard enough to know what to do and had returned to the kitchen before her ultra-caring kith and kin had left for the greenhouse. She grabbed the letter from the table and quickly made her way upstairs, bolting the lavatory door behind her.

She tore the letter into three fragments and dropped them into the lavatory pan. She then let some absorbent bum-tissue settle over it. This weighed the subject matter down. Nevertheless, it was necessary for her to flush the toilet twice before all traces of the letter had disappeared. 'That's the only fit place for shit,' thought Paula, and washed her hands most thoroughly after completing the operation. Not that she thought she could cleanse her hands entirely, as the particular faeces she had been thinking of was not the letter or its contents but her mother and aunt. Paula smiled bitterly – it would take quite a bit of ingenuity to get those two into the sewer pipe. As things stood, even that system would reject them.

'You can take your pick. There are primulas, strepto-carpus, portulaca, nierembergia and nemophilla.' The sticky heat in the greenhouse had caused Eileen to perspire. Her armpits felt particularly vulnerable as the woollen material of her jersey dress made her itch. She could hardly scratch herself where she needed to without being vulgar. There were so many plants in bloom or about to bloom. Eileen felt most uncomfortable as the names Barbara reeled off with such rapidity had no bearing on the ordered trays of plants in the glasshouse. Most of the names Barbara had used sounded more like medical terms or diseases than the names of flowers. Eileen assuaged her ignorance by taking hold of the largest of the plants, which had shiny, dark green leaves and rather lovely speckled blooms of white and red.

'This one looks healthy,' said Eileen.

'I'm afraid that's a camellia, dear; you're going a bit beyond your brief.'

'Pardon?'

'I'd let you have it, but it's the only one we have and Eric is especially attached to it. If I parted with that, it would break Eric's heart. He's so fond of it. Here, take this, it's just coming into blossom, and if you water it every three days, it will flower for months.' Barbara relieved Eileen of the camellia and passed her another pot. 'It's a cyclamen,' she said.

'I know.' Eileen could not disguise the trace of pique that had crept into her voice. 'I've seen them in Woolworths.' Anxious not to upset Barbara, she camouflaged her disappointment by quickly adding, 'Although I've never seen one this colour – or in such a lovely condition!'

Barbara smiled graciously and their former organized, sisterly warmth was revived. Like everything else, their generosity was carefully orchestrated.

These calculated appraisals of one another were to be their undoing. Barbara had thought that Eileen had been conscientious and pocketed Lydia's letter. In turn, Eileen had the utmost faith that Barbara had carefully filed away the correspondence. In their attempts to be polite, neither of them questioned the other about its whereabouts. Barbara linked her arm with her sister-in-law and escorted her to the front gate. They parted with endearments, smiles and hugs, quite unaware of the fact that their shred of sisterly conspiracy was travelling down the drainpipes beneath their feet.

10

Like the vixen she had described in her letter, Lydia had reached a point at which she felt she no longer had the resources to keep her hunters at bay. It was February, a cold, drab month, and Lydia looked forward to the warmer weather of springtime which might hold promise for her and Benny to embark on more expeditions farther beyond their home fronts. Therefore, in order not to impede her springtime time-table, she had decided on a confrontation with her children. She had talked with them on the telephone and managed to be evasive without lying. She had not seen them since her Christmas holiday and felt a little guilty that she had not missed seeing them. Paula's information as to plots to prove her insanity had not frightened or unnerved her. They had merely strengthened her resolve. It was time to go to earth.

Lydia decided to meet the pack on her own ground. Barbara had been insistent, almost to the point of being rude, that they meet in Hertfordshire. Derek had complained how inconvenient it was for him and Eileen to journey from Surrey to Lydia's home in Inner London. Lydia was reciprocally insistent with Barbara and just apologized for the inconvenience to Derek. Consequently she had prepared a high tea for her visitors, who were expected at 4.30. She had left the gas fires on in the lounge and the dining-room – a warm house might help to de-frost relationships a little.

On the Wednesday of the previous week a young man with a beard and wild, curly hair had called on her. He was dressed in jeans and a heavy woollen pullover, and a shabby duffle coat of the kind worn by workmen on building-sites protected him from the cold. This coat was studded with badges. At first, Lydia had thought he was one of the council workmen, as there had been problems with litter and rubbish-collection. Then she thought he might be a telephone engineer – she noticed that he wore one earring. Just a simple wire piercing one lobe – perhaps he was an artist? As things turned out, he was a representative of the social services and, indeed, introduced himself as a social worker. He showed Lydia a card with his photograph and credentials stamped on it. He said that his supervisor had asked him to call. The warnings from Paula ought to have made Lydia feel nervous or, at least, cautious, but the appearance of the man hardly threatened officialdom, and it was not in her nature to leave him standing out there on the step in the cold.

She invited him in and gave him tea and cake. She did not find it difficult to talk to him. He was a very engaging young man and had been in the job for one year after studying for three years at a Polytechnic. Lydia's greatest asset was her capacity for listening and she was most sympathetic as she heard of the strain of work he was expected to cover and the seemingly heavy and insurmountable problems of a varying nature that he had to patch or solve. After an hour she was beginning to wonder whether or not he had come to recruit her for some voluntary community work of one kind or another. His first and only personal question was delivered as she gave him a second piece of cake.

'I believe your family feel that you have a problem. They say they are concerned.'

'I have a lover, if you consider that a problem,' she replied promptly. She told him about Benny.

'I have to go now, Mrs Poulton.' He reached for his duffle coat. 'It's been great meeting you, and I can't say that about most of the people I have to see.'

'Do I have a problem?'

'Nope. I envy you. I just can't get a formative relationship going myself at the moment. Just can't get it together, somehow. As for your family, don't let them destroy you. There's nothing wrong with you, at all. It seems to me that if anybody needs help it's them, not you. There's no question of you being placed on my caseload.'

'Caseload?' asked Lydia.

'Oh, that's what they call the numbers of people and families I visit. Individually we call them clients.'

'My hairdresser calls me a client. Funny, that, isn't it?'

Lydia's comment had made the young man laugh. She felt he ought to laugh more often – poor boy. Before he left her, she gave him useful hints as to how to preserve his energy and one or two tips on working on formative relationships. He had not called again since, and in a way she was sorry. She had liked him so.

It was after 4.30. Lydia looked out from the lounge window. The sky had been low, leaden and grey all day. The freezing cold of the morning had not abated with the onset of the afternoon, and it had begun to snow. The flakes were large. There was no breeze. The snow was bound to settle. The inclement weather did not deter her visitors. She saw Derek's car pull in to the curbside. Her four most immediate relatives climbed from the vehicle. Lydia took a deep breath and went to the front door to welcome them.

Her children's smiles were as leaden as the sky had been, but Lydia did not let this reception chill her. She ushered them into the dining-room, clucking brightly like some contented hen over her fractious chicks. It was left to Barbara to open the agenda. She did so before any of them had taken a slice from the delicious veal loaf which Lydia had taken great pains to prepare.

'We believe you have had a visitor, Mumsy. A visitor recently.' Barbara had never called Lydia anything but 'Mother'. This term 'Mumsy' in its new setting made Lydia feel like an old lady who meandering, her mind and body away, whilst sitting in a bath chair.

'Oh, I've had a number of visitors, dear. That's why I haven't been coming over of a weekend. My time has been so full.' Lydia sliced the veal loaf as she spoke and placed generous portions in front of her guests.

'Haven't you had a special one? An official visit?' Barbara triplicated the question with her head, by lifting it slightly to one side, and with her hand, by laying one on Lydia's hand and restraining her from ministering food about the table. Barbara required direct attention, direct answers. Lydia withdrew her hand and continued to serve the food as she spoke.

'Oh, you mean the nice young man from the social

services. Gary Jones was his name. Yes, he did call, just
once, I'm afraid. I would love to see him again but his
caseload was full, and in any event I don't have any
credentials that would allow me to be placed on it. If I can fit
it in, though, I might be seeing him on Tuesday evenings.
He said that he would like me to, and I would like to help
him out. Such a nice young man – but he does look
care-worn for his age.'

'Helping him out?' Some tomato fell from Eileen's
mouth. She licked a few pips from her bottom lip.

'Well, dear, they're short of well-adjusted, liberal-
minded people of my age. That's what I am: well adjusted.
At least, that's what he says I am, and he says that I'm
non-judgemental. I've no reason to disbelieve him. It's
never been pointed out to me before. He said I would be
very useful for his group therapy meeting of ex-mental
hospital patients. He holds it on a Tuesday evening, and he
says that, in my way, I would have as much to offer as a
psychiatrist.'

'He must be bloody mad,' said Derek.

'Oh, I don't think so. He couldn't be mad and do his job.
Perhaps he might have to be a little mad in order to do it. I
don't know. Anyway, I'll probably help him out and just
see how things go. If I do have skills that will help people,
then, I should use them. Gary said that all I had to do was be
myself, and that's not difficult. More veal, Eric? You look a
little pale.'

For some reason Eric had quite suddenly begn to feel
threatened.

'Well, Mother, I think you should know that it was we
who contacted the social services. Er-er, we all felt that you
needed some kind of help yourself, er . . .' Barbara's voice
faltered. She floundered and Eileen could only support her
by nodding vigorously with her head.

'Did you, dear? I wonder why? I've never been so contented in all my life.' Lydia smiled and chewed some meat.

'Mother, I hate to say this. I really hate to say it – but your
letter from Lyme Regis just led us to believe that you were –
er – not quite yourself,' said Barbara.

'Well, we all change, dear. We're not marionettes.' Lydia

helped herself to a piece of bread and butter. Much as she disliked the prospect, she knew that it was now her time to attack. 'If the letter worried you, let's have a look at it. Where is it? To be truthful, I can't remember much that I wrote now. It was a lovely holiday. I can't think why the letter should have worried you or what you found odd or strange about it.'

An awkward silence ensued. Lydia's two female protagonists waited for their opposite number to produce the incriminating document. After a few minutes Eric coughed and gently nudged Barbara. Derek tapped Eileen on the knee. Both women remained mute and immobile, until paranoid thoughts entered Eileen's head. What if Barbara had engineered all this in order to cause a rift between her own family and Lydia? If anything happened to Lydia, would all the spoils go to Eric and Barbara? The physical semaphore of silent communication was intensified by Eileen, who kicked Barbara's shin, which was opposite her foot under the table. This action was more vehement than was intended, and caused Barbara to cry out with pain.

'Ouch, oh,' cried Barbara. Eileen glared at her sister-in-law, and Barbara lost her usual degree of composure. In an instant, she had thrown the luke-warm dregs of her tea cup into Eileen's neckline. It was left to Lydia to defuse and calm the mayhem that followed these outbursts. Some twenty minutes later, she had them all sitting. Eileen had stopped crying and Barbara's sulking had subsided. The two men, like true cowards, were glad of any kind of truce.

'My dears, you both need a good rest,' said Lydia. 'I don't think either of you realizes the intense pressures you are under, and someone has to point it out to you.' Now it's my turn, thought Lydia. 'Eileen, you never have time to be still, what with bringing up the boys, running a home and keeping Derek looking so smart. I don't think you give yourself time for a pause. All this pressure just creeps up on you, and before you know where you are, you are in tears. And you know what's the next step after that, if you let it go too far. It's the doctor and then Valium tablets – not that I've been through it, but I know people who have and I can see the signs.' Eileen blinked at Lydia's prediction that she was in the primary stage of becoming a nervous wreck. She was not at all sure that Lydia had spoken untruthfully and, full of self-pity, she began to cry.

'There, there, dear, better out than in. Derek?' Lydia glanced at her son, who dutifully comforted his wife by placing his arm about her shoulder. He might as well have been comforting an injured rugby-player. Sadly, he was like his father, as far as feelings were concerned. Somehow his feelings were pickled and there was not much one could do about that.

Lydia turned her attention to Barbara, who felt as though she were about to enter a class of fifty difficult children with a completely unprepared lesson.

'Barbara, it's time you spent some time at home. Paula was barely eight months old when you started teaching again, and you gave yourself no time to enjoy your own baby. You were much too pre-occupied, busying yourself with everybody else's children. And you still do. You've been teaching now for twenty years; why not give yourself a break? An interlude?'

'Mother, I'm a head of department, now, apart from enjoying my work. There is the economic side of things to look at. I think you are a bit out of touch with how much mortgage payments absorb, and Eric and I are forced to keep two cars . . .'

'Oh, I know all that, dear. It's just a question of what you might think you can give up on one level and gain on another. I know you love your flowers and plants and bushes and things – but it does seem excessive to spend £500 a year on them. I'm not decrying or maligning your interests but sometimes I think you verge on the obsessional about all those plants. As I've said, dear, a little pause might do you good. Perhaps it might help you to look at the quality of your life. More tea, dear?'

Barbara was flabbergasted and couldn't answer her mother. She had never heard her speak in such a manner. What did Lydia mean by quality? There ought to have been a set answer to Lydia's observations but Barbara could think of nothing to say – or rather, she was afraid to reply in case Lydia might reveal more pertinent insights which lay in the recesses of Barbara's being. She did not wish to be confronted with them. Being busy was more comfortable. Barbara remained silent and sipped her tea. Eric glanced at his wife and, surprisingly, felt no pity for her. Their marriage had been based on competing with one another. They discussed things together, yet in spite of a satisfactory marriage, he did not feel that he and his wife were friends. She had even begun to dress like him – as for the economics, she was earning more than he now, and from time to time she gently reminded him of this fact.

Eileen felt much better after listening to Lydia's remarks concerning Barbara. It was about time somebody put her sister-in-law down – clever-arsed know-all. Eileen interpreted this as Barbara being out of favour. She was quick to make amends to her mother-in-law.

'It was Barbara's idea from the first, Mummy. I never liked it from the first. I really didn't feel the need to interfere with your, er, private life, but . . .'

'That's not ture. It's not true, you . . .' Barbara lost control and screamed.

'My dears, it's all been a misunderstanding, and neither of you is to blame. So please don't quarrel about it any more. As you've said, we are a family, and I'll help both you all I can.'

'You've changed, Mother,' said Derek.

'No, dear, I haven't. Mr Jones (the social worker) said that I was declaring my identity. It's been buried for a long time. Now that I am using it, I shall probably appear a little different but I'm not. I'm awake. I'm sure you understand things a bit more clearly now.'

Eric found himself stunned with admiration and was searching his heart for a considered but not effusive compliment. Before he could put his contribution into words, the door bell rang.

'This is my friend Benny.' Lydia held his arm as she introduced him to her guests. Benny did not seem in the slightest ill at ease. He smiled and nodded. The four guests, astonished by their mother's audacity and boldness, returned his greeting with monosyllabic grunts and smiles that hid their alarm and trepidation. It would have been right and proper to commence a formal but friendly conversation. However, the group were still in an individual state of shock. They remained the pivot of the proceedings. Lydia brought them to consciousness by yet another verbal dose of smelling salts. She glanced at her wristwatch.

'Well, dears, I have to shoo you away now. I hadn't realized we'd all been here so long. It's well after six and we've made arrangements to go out. I'm sure you won't mind. It's stopped snowing, but I'm sure you won't want to get home too late.' She turned to Benny. 'I hope it's not cancelled.'

'We'll take a chance,' he said.

'We're going to the dogs,' Lydia declared.

'Mother, you always used to say that you could never be interested in pets. You never even kept a cat. How can you think of going to a dog show on a night like this?'

Eric wished his wife would keep her mouth shut. She wasn't as clever as she thought she was. Lydia frowned.

'Not a dog show, dear. We are going to the White City. It's a dog track, greyhound racing. It's very comfortable where we sit. You can have a bet for 10p and watch the dogs race from the bar. I usually have two glasses of port and lemon. When the lights go down, it's very exciting and really very colourful and pretty. I'd recommend the experience. It's not expensive. Much cheaper than a dinner and dance. You can't lose a lot of money if you only place 10p on each race. Just go for the entertainment, as we do.'

'Sounds like a good idea.' Eric managed to speak. Barbara's shoulders jerked back as though a spear had struck her between the shoulder blades.

'I'll go along with you one night.' Derek hated dinner-dances. Nobody at the bank was likely to see him at a dog track. He wouldn't have to wear a suit.

Swift, polite farewells were exchanged. After her relatives had left, Benny helped Lydia into her fur coat.

'The first hare runs at 7.30,' he said.

'The dogs never catch it, do they, Benny?' Lydia asked.

'Oh, no, darlin', they never catch the hare.'

'I'm glad about that,' said Lydia.

11

'Oh, dear God, I must have dialled three noughts. I must put my finger in the second hole. I want three nines. Yes, I must dial three nines. Try again. Keep calm.' Lydia placed her index finger in the second hole from the end and concentrated on spinning the dial round. The voice that answered her was impersonal. She couldn't really expect it to be anything else.

'Emergency, which service please?'

'There's been an accident. I wonder if . . .'

'What do you require? Police, fire or ambulance?'

'Oh, er, ambulance, and I suppose police. Are police helpful for next of kin?'

'Your address?' Lydia gave Benny's address and waited for information.

'I'll put you through to ambulance and the police. Are you there, madam?'

'Yes, I am here.' Lydia was informed by both public services that they would call immediately. She placed the receiver down, tightened the belt on her dressing-gown and ascended the stairs.

'Benny,' she called as she entered the bathroom. There was no logic in her calling out his name. Her lips had moved and the sound had come out. He lay there next to the sink on the linoleum floor. This was where she had found him earlier. She had gone downstairs to make a pot of tea and some toast. He had said he would shave first. She was afraid the tea would get stewed and the toast go cold. It was unlike Benny to take a bath in the morning. She called up to him and he had not replied. The attack must have occurred whilst he was shaving. The razor had slipped during his seizure and consequent contortion. Blood trickled from a small but deep wound on the left side of his neck. No sniffers or kisses could bring him back to life. Lydia had not got too close to him but had telephoned immediately.

'Oh, Benny.' She spoke again and knelt at his side. The glazed eyes, the congealed blood that covered his neck and besmirched his pyjama jacket, the spittle at the corners of his twisted mouth caused her no revulsion. She approached him practically, tenderly, as though she were preparing his breakfast. If she talked, she wouldn't cry. She did not want to cry and provided herself with a commentary which was private to Benny and her.

'The toast has gone cold, dear, but I'll make some fresh pieces.' Lydia took a face cloth from the sink and soaked it in water. She wiped the blood from his neck and chest and smoothed down his few strands of hair, then ruffled the hair, then smoothed it down again.

'I'll make another pot of tea, dearest heart. We'll have a slow breakfast.' She removed the froth and spittle from his mouth and closed his jaws. Then there were his eyes, so blue, so blue. 'I'll draw the curtains for you.' She closed the lids and remained kneeling at his side after she had straightened his legs. She remained like this and continued talking.

'Well, you've gone now, Benny, gone from me in the late springtime of the year – but what a time we had.'

Lydia began to button his pyjama jacket, not that he was likely to catch a cold now but Benny always liked to look proper. She gazed at his hairy chest. The curly hairs were white-tipped as though sprinkled with hoar frost. For Lydia, they had always been an unaccountable attraction. She had always been excited by them since her first sighting and touch. She touched them once more, for the last time, before fastening the top button of his pyjama jacket. It was impossible not to make parallels. Her husband's death she had accepted – yes, if she were truthful, ignored. But sitting with her lover she could neither accept nor ignore the finality. She had never fainted in her life, although there were times when she had wished she could. What she was experiencing was the nearest thing to a coma that one could experience without losing any of one's sensibilities. She had not had an injection of morphine, yet she felt no pain, numbed perhaps, but aware.

She left him and returned with two cups of tea. She

placed his cup beside him and sat on the floor, rested her back against the wall and drank her own. Ritual could be private, and this was her way of honouring him. No one could understand it. It was none of their business, anyway.

'You know, Paula ended her relationship with the young man from Wolverhampton. He came round. He was most upset. His face has always had a fixed look, but he looked more tired than ever. He asked if he could come out with us this afternoon. I said yes. It seemed a strange request. He didn't say why he and Paula had parted company, and I didn't think it right to ask why. I mean, if he had wanted to tell me, he would have done. He said he'd like to continue to keep in contact with us in spite of him and Paula going their separate ways. I said he would always be welcome. Do you think that was right of me, Benny?'

The inert body did not reply. A little more blood trickled down from the wound. Lydia took this as an affirmative to her question.

Before she could converse any more, a fierce banging broke her reverie. She carried her half-drunk cup of tea with her, and opened the door.

Aid, or whatever one could term it in the circumstances, had come quickly, simultaneously. The police car had drawn up behind the ambulance which was parked with expert precision with its rear at the curbside facing the door.

'Upstairs, the second turning on the left.' Lydia indicated the direction to the fresh-faced ambulance men. She left the door ajar and followed behind them. The older of the two men was bending over Benny. Lydia stood in the doorway of the bathroom. The ambulance man glanced up to her, met her gaze.

'I'm afraid there's nothing we can do. He's gone. He's dead, Mrs . . . er.'

'Poulton.'

'Yes, I'm sorry, dear. He's dead . . .'

'I know, but I can't believe it, yet.' Lydia finished off her tea and placed the cup on the floor.

The two policemen had stood respectfully behind. One of them stepped forward and looked at the blood.

'Was your husband worried about anything, Mrs

Poulton?' he asked. Before Lydia could answer, he had taken out a notebook and questioned her again. 'Was there any history of mental disturbance, depression, anything like that? I mean, can you think of any reason why he should wish to take his own life?'

'Three questions,' murmured Lydia.

'I beg your pardon, madam.' The policeman's voice had hardened and his biro remained poised over his notebook.

'You have asked me three questions,' said Lydia as she pulled the scarlet blanket over Benny's body which the ambulance men had deftly but tenderly transferred to the stretcher.

'He is not, he was not, my husband.'

'You were his housekeeper?' The policeman's voice had almost become metallic.

'His lover,' said Lydia. 'We have separate houses but we have commuted for the past few months. It has been a very satisfactory arrangement. We have been very happy. He has not been depressed. On the contrary, he has been joyous. There is no reason why he could want to take away his own life. He had every reason to preserve it.'

The ambulance man cut through any more of the sinister implications and probing which had dropped all traces or veneers of comfort. He spoke to the policeman sharply.

'This man has died from natural causes – a heart attack. It's quite clear. The hospital will verify the facts. You can contact them if you have any doubts. A mouse couldn't die from this neck wound. He'd been shaving when the seizure hit him. You can ask for an autopsy if you want to make idiots of yourselves.'

Lydia looked at the uniformed quartet. The police withdrew and left without condolence; they took facts from Lydia, just facts. The ambulance men accepted a cup of tea. There was little need to rush. When they left, they patted her head and shoulders, sensing that words would not convey solace or comfort.

The seventeenth of May, and summer had not even begun. Lydia looked at the calendar: Thursday 17 May. She sat for an hour, perhaps more, and then got up mechanically. Like some robot she began to hoover, scrub, polish every part of Benny's home. Curtains were taken down that did not need washing and were placed in the boiler. Windows were cleaned inside and out. Relentlessly she kept working. Cleansing, cleaning, she kept moving, inventing domestic tasks where none existed. She was polishing the stair rail for the second time when Stephen arrived at 3 p.m. She let him into the house and then collapsed. Slumped and inert she sat at the foot of the stairs, still clad in her pink dressing-gown. The belt had come awry so that one of her heavy breasts was totally exposed. She held the duster in one hand and pushed something away from her eyes with the other as though some heavy cobwebs were clutching at her or impairing her vision. Stephen's immediate impression was that Lydia was suffering from some kind of temporary blindness.

'Benny died this morning. I've been cleaning the house. I forgot about you coming. I've been cleaning and . . .'

Stephen helped her to her feet and ushered her onto the settee in the lounge. He sat her down very carefully, lifted up her legs and placed a cushion behind her head as though he were packing some precious piece of luggage. She was unaware that he also tucked her breast in and fastened her dressing-gown. He sat on the floor beside her and said nothing. He remained there for some time. Lydia asked nothing of him. She did not ask him to leave or to stay. He was not, nor ever had been, equipped to deal with emergencies but all he could think of was that he did not want to leave her alone. The telephone rang. Lydia remained on the settee. She did not appear to hear the telephone's insistent ringing. Stephen answered the call.

'Yes, yes, it's quite all right. Yes, you may return it here. Yes, there will be someone to receive it. Thank you.' He returned to Lydia and spoke bluntly. 'They are bringing Benny's body back from the hospital. His GP was contacted. He had told them it is miraculous that Benny has gone on for so long.'

'So long?' Lydia asked, thinking of their few months together. Now that Stephen had got her talking, he sought to break the odd trance-like stupor into which Lydia had retreated. It was necessary for her to accept what had happened and not obliterate or cushion herself from the morning's events. He had observed that Lydia was often at her best when she was being practical. Therefore he confronted her brutally, compassionately, with what was to be expected of her.

'Death by natural causes. Apparently his heart was as good as defunct more than a year ago. He carried a card that gave information if anything happened to him while he was out. Did you know that?'

'Oh, yes,' said Lydia, as she drew her legs off the settee and sat facing Stephen, her hands clasped together. She felt the need to hold her hands in case they started fluttering about. It was as though they had become nervous sparrows, not part of her. They wanted to flutter, and she could sense her own trembling.

'You'll need some help,' said Stephen. Lydia looked questioningly at him. 'There are arrangements to be made, next of kin to be contacted, his solicitor, his doctor, the undertaker . . .'

'Where do I begin?' Lydia stood.

'You begin by getting dressed. Then I suggest we move one of the single beds into this room.' His reply was cool but sweetly considered, and Lydia nodded and obeyed the young man from Wolverhampton. She took a bath, dressed, applied her make-up and splashed on some Lily of the Valley.

Stephen had managed to get the single bed from the spare room down into the living-room whilst she was carrying out her ablutions. He had also placed clean white sheets and a pillow in their correct positions. Lydia was busy making telephone calls when the body arrived. Stephen directed the operations as to its placement. When this was done, he placed the kettle to boil for some tea and waited for Lydia to join him in the kitchen. She was a long time talking. He could hear her voice. He was surprised at its clarity; questions were asked, details were given and he did not detect any tremor or breaking of modulation or tone. Given a sense of purpose, Mrs Poulton was a very strong lady. No wonder Benny had lived beyond his time –

her kind of strength would have deterred leprosy, let alone a 'dicky' heart.

Stephen placed a mug of tea in her hands. She drank a little.

'He seems to have made all his own arrangements. All I had to do was confirm them. His solicitor even knew the name and address of the undertaker he wanted. Someone in the Whitechapel Road. The burial, even the burial, is paid for. I have to visit the solicitor tomorrow morning. According to the solicitor, he nominated me as his sole next of kin. It's a nice phrase – next of kin.' Lydia smiled and drank a little more tea.

'Didn't he have any other relatives? I mean blood relations?'

'Yes, an unmarried sister but she died last year. His wife was an orphan so there is no one on her side. No, the solicitor was adamant. I'm his next of kin. I'm his wife, his mother, his daughter. 'I'm . . .' Lydia began to cry. Stephen was relieved to witness the tears.

'Let it rip for a bit. Go on, let yourself go.' He offered a rather dirty khaki handkerchief, and Lydia gave her nose a thorough, heavy blow.

'Thanks, I feel better now,' she said. 'Would you like a tomato sandwich? I have some cake as well. You must be hungry.' She had already opened the kitchen cabinet, and Stephen was hungry. He let her get on with it.

'You may as well finish it off.' Lydia was referring to the last chunk of cake. She had been talking while the young man was eating.

He swallowed her reminiscences with his food. Most of them were simple anecdotes of exploits she had shared with Benny. Her last comment caused a piece of cake to stick in his throat and startled him a little. 'And what a lover he was, what a lover, oh, he could make love.' She concluded her own 'In Memoriam' with these words. He gulped some of the tea to help the cake down. For some reason her perfume, that heavy smell, whirred about his head, and his mind pondered over the large breast that he had placed technically back into position in the earlier part of the day. He recovered himself quickly by placing his empty plate, cup and saucer in a neat pile before him.

'Do you want me to contact your family?' he asked.

'My family?'

'Yes, Derek, Barbara, Eileen and Eric.' He had got the couples in the wrong order.

'No. No, I'll tell them, but not yet. Not until I'm ready.' Lydia spoke decisively.

'What about Paula?' Stephen faltered over her grand-daughter's name.

'I think Paula is best left for the moment. Best left to herself. I'll tell her when I tell the others.' Lydia was surprised at Stephen's outburst at this remark.

'Whatever she is, she's not left to herself. She's living with one of the college lecturers. He's a sociologist, fast-talker, brilliant. He doesn't treat her well. Have you ever felt jealous, Mrs Poulton?'

'No, I don't think I've ever experienced it.'

'You're lucky,' he said.

'Do you think so?' said Lydia. Sadness had crept into her voice. Stephen detected it, and discarded his self-indulgence.

'Is there anything more I can do to help you? Do you want me to see you home?' He looked downcast, poor boy, thought Lydia. He's lost a lover, too. Perhaps it was easier to lose them in the way she had lost Benny.

'No, I'm staying here, dear. I shall be staying here until everything is complete. This is my home, too – oh, er.' Her pause was contrived.

'Yes?'

'It's only a suggestion, but if you wish . . . if you wouldn't find it a hindrance, you could look after my own house for the next few weeks or so. No rent, of course, just as a guest to keep the place warm and lived in. I suppose your accommodation is fixed by the college, is it?'

'No, in the second and third years we just find our own places and pay the rent out of our grant. A stay at your place would help me a lot financially.'

Lydia was well aware of this fact but had subtly chosen not to essay her offer to him as a favour. She collected her handbag and gave him the keys. He held them in his hand and bit his lower lip. Lydia was waiting for him to leave. She wished to be alone now. Stephen remained and the silence between them would have soon reached tension proportions if Lydia had left him standing there with the keys of her house in the palm of his hand.

'Is anything the matter?' she asked him.

'If Paula should call round, or if she telephones . . .'

'Then tell her I'm here,' Lydia interrupted.

'You see, I don't want to see her. I don't want to see her. It still hurts me, Mrs Poulton.'

'Yes, I know it does, dear – but it will go away eventually.'

'What?'

'The hurt.'

He buttoned his jacket and held out his hand for her to shake, as he had shaken hands with a referee at a football match. What a small hand she had, almost like a child's. Stephen was not impulsive or demonstrative by nature so that his next action surprised him as much as it did Lydia. He pulled her to him and hugged her quite hard. Indeed, Lydia had to catch her breath a little as his encircling arms squeezed her to him. He left saying that he would telephone in a couple of days time, together with the assurance that she could contact him if need be. A new friend, thought Lydia as she closed the door behind him.

Immediately she made her way into the lounge where her old friend lay. The white sheet was drawn over his head and shoulders, so that all she could make out were the contours of the human frame that lay beneath the coverlet. She was not tempted to lift the sheet and look at Benny's face. She no longer needed to be convinced that he was dead. From her handbag she took out her bottle of Lily of the Valley. She had used over half its content already. She let the rest of the perfume drip onto the white coverlet, a spottle here, a spottle there, so that the heavy aroma was all about him.

Afterwards she sat at the other end of the lounge. She found that her hands belonged to her again. She began to read one of her 'shocking' novels. From time to time, she would place her book down and glance towards Benny and then resume her reading. She was quite calm, quite still.

In this way Lydia commenced her grieving. Grief of this kind was new to her, and she accepted it like a journey into the unknown, not seeking to interpret the intensity of its cause or wanting to know the outcome of its effect. As for sharing what she felt with anyone, that was quite out of the question.

Christabel, the main character in her present reading-material, was bound and gagged and locked in the huge refrigerator of a butcher who had offered the girl romance which had turned horribly sour. Now the heroine was in a fridge. At least I'm warm, thought Lydia as she drew the curtains together across the front window.

12

'I thought the summer would never come.'

Barbara waved away a bee that had drifted from draining the honey from one of her roses and begun to hover above her brow.

'Yes, it's almost too hot, now, although I suppose we shouldn't complain. It's the end of June and we've barely had the opportunity to sit out like this.'

Eileen made an attempt to lie back in her deckchair. There was not a lot of room on the tiny patch of lawn that Barbara had left like an island in the sea of assorted roses which made up her back garden.

Their respective husbands sat opposite their wives. There was no space for a fifth chair. Paula curled herself cat-like on the grass beside her father's chair. She rested her elbows on the edge of its wooden frame.

'Well, it looks as though Mother had more sense than we gave her credit for,' said Derek.

'What do you mean?' Eric knew full well what his brother-in-law meant but chose to keep up an appearance of sensitivity. In his way he was more callous in that he chose to hide behind the real reason for the present gathering. He breathed in deeply, conscious of his roses and hopefully giving an introduction to someone to comment on them. He would have liked the conversation to drift towards Lydia gently. Direct approaches had failed in the past.

Derek was under no such constraint. His mother had been reasonably well off before Benny's death. As things now stood, she was what could be termed a wealthy woman. From all accounts she had been left a considerable amount of money as well as a house that was larger than the one she already owned. Property never devalued, and Lydia's new abode (she had chosen to move into Benny's house) was situated in an area of London which was just becoming fashionable. Prices were rocketing in the area, and houses that had once belonged to artisans were now being avidly sought by highly paid businessmen and professional workers on high salaries. Brass door-knockers were being placed on many of the doors, and central heating firms were enjoying a bonanza in installation fees.

'You know quite well what I mean, and don't pretend that you haven't thought about it.'

'I'm not looking at money all day.' Eric sounded petulant, and Barbara winced at his reply. More and more she considered her husband a weak man. This tended to put her off him in more ways than one. She often chose to hurt him, but he seemed immune to her barks or her restraint in bed. She glanced in his direction, challenging him to speak further. He lowered himself further into his deckchair, closed his eyes and cupped his hand above his brow, feigning a pretence of shielding his eyes from the sun's glare. 'So it's left to me again,' thought Barbara.

'Yes, you're quite right, Derek, Mother does have a lot of responsibility.' This was her way of referring to Lydia's wealth. 'Obviously it's a great strain on her, otherwise she would have contacted us more often.'

'Yes,' Eileen interrupted. 'I mean, none of us knew of the man's death, the funeral, nothing. She kept the whole thing bottled up to herself for weeks. We had a real shock, I can tell you, when we called round to see her. A real shock. Fancy a total stranger opening the front door to us. I'll never forget it, never. And the way he treated us, in our own mother's house. "I'm one of Mrs Poulton's tenants," he said. He spoke as though he was God Almighty and looked as though he were a tramp.'

'He's the social worker – Gary Jones – you all sent him to Gran,' Paula giggled. Eileen ignored her.

'Apparently, there are two more tenants in the house besides him. One of them, I'm sure, is his girl-friend. The other is another man. He just would not volunteer any information about what financial arrangements had been made. "Ask your mother" was all he would say. I found him rude, yes, quite rude. He said that the other tenants were out, so we've no idea who they are, not even their names. He had the cheek to ask me to telephone before I chose to call again.'

'He was perfectly within his rights,' said Eric.

'Thank God Mother left the house furnished,' said Derek.

Barbara sat up and crossed her legs, placed her hands in her lap and took on the air of composure of the person who knows what to say and do next.

'I think it would be very silly of us to appear to be pushing Mother as to the way things are at the moment. The last time we met her – that is, as a group – I think she possibly interpreted our concern – or, if you like, our love for her – as some sort of disapproval.'

'It was,' said Paula.

'Shut up. Now we have to show Mother that we approve. We have to make some kind of magnanimous gesture of help that is impossible for her to reject.'

'It's a bit difficult, when she's refusing to see us,' said Derek.

'I'm sure she hardly ever, if ever, goes out of the house now, except to buy food,' said Eileen somewhat wearily.

'Eileen, you have hit the nail on the head,' said Barbara.

Eileen smiled and tried to cover up her puzzlement. She did not know what nail or what head Barbara was talking about. Barbara took a large envelope from the straw basket which lay at her feet. She extracted a coloured brochure from the envelope and held it aloft.

'Mother needs a holiday. A holiday abroad. And my suggestion is . . . that we pay for it.'

'Oh, dear, I'm not sure . . .'

Derek interrupted his wife. 'Yes, yes, a sensible investment,' he said.

'Investment!' Paula cried.

'Shush, Paula,' said her father.

'Well, it won't work because she won't see any of us. If we send her a ticket, there is no guarantee that she will use it, and then the money and effort will have been wasted.'

Barbara nodded agreement at Eileen's observation. The group looked rather crestfallen and glum.

'There is one of us she *will* see.' Eric spoke quietly.

All the adults looked towards Paula. She stood.

'I won't go. I won't go. I want no part of it.'

Even as she spoke she took the brochure from her mother's hands and began to glean the details and delights that a fortnight on the Costa Brava could offer her grandmother.

Paula arrived at Lydia's new home to find her grandmother playing cribbage with Bunty. She was received cordially and was asked if she would mind waiting a bit until they had finished their hand. This gave Paula time to browse about the house. It had been suggested by her parents that her grandmother had refused to see them because she was overcome with grief and had entered a state of withdrawal quite common in such cases. As she wandered from room to room, she quickly concluded that for the first time Lydia had imprinted her own taste on her new accommodation. Fussy, chintz curtains decorated the windows. The walls were not papered but all were adorned in pretty, light, pastel colours. Small cushions seemed to pop up like mushrooms everywhere. None of Benny's belongings or furniture had been removed, but all, in the most curious ways, had been decorated or titivated. It was as though Lydia were impregnating his possessions with her being.

'I'm out,' Paula heard her grandmother cry triumphantly, and correctly assumed that the cribbage game was over. She entered the lounge, and Lydia's guest stood to greet her formally.

'This is my friend Mr Burford. He runs the "Know Your City" class. Bunty, my grand-daughter Paula.' Lydia did not seem withdrawn. On the contrary she was relaxed – yes, even gracious. Paula sat and joined them. Lydia carefully gathered the cards together, removed the peg-board and placed them on a shelf.

'I can see where Lydia gets her looks.' Mr Burford spoke directly to Paula and fingered a decorated tooth or fang which hung from his neck on a silver chain.

'You've got it the wrong way round, surely?' Paula realized that she was sounding like her own mother.

'What, dear?' Mr Burford asked vaguely.

'Well, surely, if there is a resemblance between me and my gran, then it is she who passes on the likenesses to me. Chronologically speaking, it wouldn't be possible the other way around.'

Mr Burford obviously didn't feel that the topic merited any further probing. He offered Paula a cigarette, took one himself and lit them. They both inhaled.

'My friends call me Bunty,' he said as he puffed a cloud of smoke into the air.

'How are you, dear? It's ages since I last saw you. Are you happy?' Lydia hoped that these open, generalized questions might spark off some sort of communication between Paula and Bunty. At the moment all they were doing was sending smoke signals to one another. They were sitting close but each had distanced the other.

'In a state of *anomie*.' Paula blew out some more smoke.

'Have you been to the doctor, dear? Do your parents know?' Lydia was genuinely fond of Paula, and the idea that her grand-daughter might be ill caused her immediate distress.

'It's not an illness,' said Bunty. Paula looked at him. 'Clever as well as camp,' she thought. She waited for him to explain the word but from either humility or innate pride he chose to remain silent and outwardly flippant. Paula had ceased to believe that she had anything to teach her grand-mother, but now she had forced herself into a situation in which she had to explain. She cursed her own pomposity but nevertheless spoke like some retarded pedagogue whose audience was no longer of any consequence to him.

'It's not easy to explain. Lawrence could explain it to you better.'

'Lawrence?'

'He's the man I am living with. He's a lecturer in sociology.'

'Oh, yes, dear.' Lydia did not enquire more. If she enquired, she would have to divulge Stephen's situation, and she felt that this would have been unfair to all concerned. Paula picked up some sewing Lydia had left on the settee. She drew the needle that had carefully been threaded into the curtain material. She removed the cotton from its eye and showed the needle to her grandmother. Conscious that she was being dramatic, Paula drove the needle into the back of her own hand. Her face contorted with pain at the impact.

'Darling, darling! Don't, Paula dear!' Lydia pleaded. She took the needle away from Paula. 'You've made yourself bleed.' Lydia took Paula's hand and surveyed the spot of blood that had bubbled onto the hand where the skin had been punctured.

Paula let her grandmother wipe away the blood. 'I take a needle, I jab my hand, yet it's as though it's not happening to me. I can feel the pain, though.' Paula licked the back of her hand.

'Yes, and the blood was there, so it did happen. I shouldn't worry too much about being in that state – what was it, dear?' Lydia asked.

'*Anomie.*'

'Yes, you mentioned it before; well, I've been in it. I think I might still be on the fringes of it, myself, but I've no blood to show for it.' Lydia re-threaded the needle and took up her sewing.

'That's why they sent me. Your children sent me along today. I would have waited for you to contact me. Can I open the window? It's a bit warm in here.' Paula made as if to stand but Bunty motioned her to sit; he rose and pushed open the back window. Paula took a large envelope from her bag. She placed it on the coffee table. Lydia stopped sewing. If it was some kind of official communication from her children, she needed concentration. She had come to regard the motives of her most immediate relatives with a high degree of suspicion.

'You can open it. It's a surprise,' said Paula. Lydia looked towards Bunty, who was still standing at the half-open window. He interpreted her glance and joined her on the settee. Lydia *was* surprised. She placed the brochures and the air tickets on the table.

'I don't understand,' she said.

'They're giving you a holiday. A holiday abroad. Three weeks on the Costa Brava,' Paula explained, flatly.

'It's for the middle of July . . .'

'Four weeks from today,' said Bunty.

'But it's not my birthday or anything like that. It really seems a most extravagant thing to do.' Lydia studied the costing of the hotel booking and flight. 'I couldn't possibly· accept it from them. It's a very kind thought but what would I do in Spain? No, I really can't accept it. I must say it's very generous. Very generous.' Lydia picked up her sewing once more.

'If you don't use the bloody thing, they might not be able to get their money returned. They would feel hurt,' said Paula.

'I don't want to hurt anyone. You could use the ticket, dear. It sounds much more suitable for you than for me . . .'

'I think you should go, Lydia, love.' Bunty crossed his legs. Paula noticed that his small feet pointed outwards. She hadn't expected him to be an ally.

'Why? It's not as though I have nothing to do with my time. All my days are full. I'm busier now than I have even been in my life. Mondays, I come to your class; Tuesdays, I go to see Mrs Arkwright, the lady with phlebitis; Wednesdays, I help with Gary's psychotherapy group at the hospital; Thursdays, I . . .'

'Benny would have liked you to have gone.' Bunty stopped Lydia in her itemized tracks. 'A holiday doesn't stop you from remembering a lover. It's an acid test. If it was real, it's with you wherever you are. Are you afraid you might forget him?'

Paula was alarmed that Bunty's shock tactics might upset Lydia. She thought he had gone too far. She watched him finger the tooth necklace. Young men of eighteen and twenty-three were wearing them – Paula did tend to think chronologically.

'As for the state you've both said you are now in, I've been in it all my life. Never had any choice in the matter. If I had any choice, I probably wouldn't be sitting here looking and talking like a preserved peacock. A fat preserved peacock.' He ended with a sigh.

'Bunty,' Paula was moved. 'Bunty, I don't know you but I think you are being unfair on yourself.' She had used his nickname, carried away by the quick flashes of compassion that she was always so anxious to conceal within herself. 'Well, Gran?' Paula asked.

'The cotton keeps falling away from the eye.' Lydia examined the needle. She sucked at the cotton so that its shattered strands were organized back to a sleek point. She threaded it through the eye of the needle on her first attempt. 'There, I've done it,' she murmured with satisfaction. 'Tell them I accept, dear. Thank them all very much for their kindness.' Having threaded the needle, she returned it to its former position in the cloth. She did not continue with her sewing. She wandered over to the window and looked out onto Benny's lawn. Dry, bald patches were beginning to appear on it.

'I've never travelled alone. At least, never any great distance.' She spoke to the lawn.

'It will be an adventure for you, darling.' Bunty sounded enthusiastic, as though he had thrown back two quick glasses of champagne.

'It might be, Gran,' Paula added, more cautiously. Lydia turned to them both.

'Well, we'll have to wait and see, won't we? Now, I'll make us all a pot of tea.'

13

Lydia held the telephone a little distance away from her ear. Barbara always spoke loudly. Lydia put it down to her daughter's years of teaching and instructing. She always spoke as if she were addressing a group, never an individual.

'I think you are being much too complacent about it, Mother. We were all angry on your behalf. We still feel that you should claim a refund. It's nonsense for them to tell you that they have over-booked at this late stage. I am sure we could have insisted on them finding you another hotel in Spain. If only you had let us know earlier. It's audacious. How can three weeks in North Africa be a substitute for a holiday on the Costa Brava?'

'Well, it's all they could offer, dear, and really, I don't mind.' Lydia held her hand over the mouthpiece so that her daughter was spared from hearing her irritated sigh. Tunisia or Spain? It didn't make any difference to Lydia. In fact, she was happier with the idea of going to Tunisia, not because of any exotic delights she thought the place might offer but mainly because Benny had been stationed there during the war, in 1942, in the very place she was now bound for. Benny had liked it.

'Have you seen your doctor? You'll need injections for all sorts of things. They give you immunity.' Barbara repeated the word, 'immunity', just in case her mother wanted to ask what it meant.

'Oh, I've had all of them, dear,' Lydia lied. She did not want to be immune. She had seen the doctor, who had only cautioned her about the drinking-water. No injections were mentioned and Lydia hated them, so she had not pursued the matter with him. Barbara prattled on about dangers from disease which, according to her, was everywhere, in everything and every person. She cautioned her mother on associations. It was right and proper to be polite to the local inhabitants but essential to remain totally formal. She was to be careful with her handbag, and check the value of her currency. She was not to travel alone in a taxi, not to buy anything from street hawkers, not to go on any trips without a guide . . . Lydia held the telephone in her lap. This stream of negation bored her. She would do as she pleased.

'Mother, Mother, are you there?'

'Yes, dear.'

'Oh, I thought we had been cut off. Now, are you sure you don't want us to get you to the airport?'

'You've been too kind already, my dear. Don't worry. I've made all the arrangements. I'll drop you a card when I've settled in. Apparently the post takes quite a time, so don't agitate yourselves if you don't hear from me the first week or so. Now, I must finish my packing. Thank you for telephoning. Give my love to everyone, won't you.' Lydia did not wait for any more dollops of sensible advice from her daughter. She placed the receiver down. If there were going to be any difficulties with regard to her trip, she now felt that the worst of them was over.

When Stephen arrived, late that afternoon, Lydia observed that he had got very thin. His clothes hung on him, and his bearded face looked drawn and haggard. He resembled the many tortured-looking saints she had looked at in art galleries and similar institutions she had visited with Bunty. Stephen had always looked older than his years, but now his gaunt appearance aged him further. The dark circles under his eyes, the lines that had appeared on his brow and the added length of his beard gave him an ancient air. Apart from his clothing he looked historical.

At his suggestion, Lydia had agreed that he should stay in her present living accommodation whilst she was away. He had said that the house shouldn't be left empty and that by staying there he could keep an eye on the place. Lydia had not believed that this was the real reason for his wishing to stay there but had agreed to his request. His long-term state of unhappiness worried her, as there was little she could do to alleviate it. She had placed a large casserole in the oven for their evening meal. At least she could feed him a little. He had insisted on driving her to the airport. He would stay with her tonight and they would leave at 7.30 in the morning. Her flight departure was scheduled for 9.30 but Stephen had pointed out the small print which indicated that all baggage should be checked in an hour before the flight. Lydia was grateful for his unfussy assistance. She had never travelled in an aeroplane before.

'You land at Monastir,' he said. They had finished their meal and he was reading through all her travel documents.

'Are you sure? I know that's not the name of the town where my hotel is. The place I'm staying in doesn't sound as attractive as that. But, then, names are misleading. 'No, that's not . . .'

'Sousse,' he said.

'Yes, that's it. Sounds odd, doesn't it? Like a soap powder or something you might use in the kitchen.'

'The travel company will get you from Monastir to Sousse. I think there are a number of resorts on that strip of coast. I shouldn't worry about it.'

Stephen had placed his knife and fork across a half-finished meal. Lydia was not worried about her itinerary but she was worried about Stephen. Adults were like babies. You couldn't force them to eat. She could hardly pat Stephen's back, as it was much more than a bit of wind that he was suffering from, but whatever it was within him that was engineering his physical decline, it had to be got out somehow.

'I thought we'd have a bottle of wine to celebrate. We should celebrate my first flight, shouldn't we?' Lydia produced a magnum bottle and two half-pint glasses. She filled Stephen's and took a much smaller measure for herself.

'Here's to your flight – to your flying.' He raised his glass and took an unusually large gulp. Half the contents had gone. He had consumed it as if it were lemonade. Lydia took a sip from her glass and watched Stephen drain the contents of his. She refilled his glass. He took another gulp.

'I'm grounded,' he said. Lydia did not choose to understand his comment but noted with a degree of satisfaction that he had taken up his fork again and begun to pick at and eat some more of his dinner.

An hour later Lydia felt that her instincts had led her to be a little wayward. Stephen was smiling quite a lot. His thin face showed the lines and crags even more when he smiled. His eyes were rather glazed. They stared at her but she was not sure whether or not he was actually seeing her. He had talked non-stop in the most animated fashion about three football teams, their rises, their declines, what the future would be for them. He was in the middle of explaining some kind of aggressive forward attacking style of play that one of the teams had adopted. Quite suddenly, he stopped.

'Fuck football!' he said, and began to cry. Lydia remained where she was, sitting opposite him. He wiped his eyes and looked at her as though he were a camera. Eventually he managed to get her into focus. 'Sorry, Mrs Poulton, sorry. I'm pissed.'

'Never mind, dear, you've eaten all your dinner.' Lydia cleared away the plates. She heard him stagger to the bathroom. He was muttering something to himself, and Lydia thought she heard a little more swearing.

'The little room is ready, Stephen. The bed is all made up,' she called up to him.

'Right, right,' he called back. She could hear him urinating.

Lydia took the precaution of telephoning the operator and asking for an early alarm call the following morning. Stephen had the clock in his room, and Lydia felt some misgivings as to the state of his consciousness the next day.

The morning arrived and she felt a little embarrassed. He had risen before her and made her a pot of tea and some toast. When the telephone did ring, she rushed to answer it and said, 'Yes, thank you, Mrs Lipton, I will.' The operator must have thought some trickster was on the line but mercifully repeated her number and Lydia repeated her phrase before he rang off. Stephen did not ask what Mrs Lipton was doing telephoning at such a strange hour. He smiled a little and poured Lydia's tea.

'I have to leave you, now,' was all he said to her at the airport.

Lydia passed through customs control with a label fastened to the lapel of her coat. Other people wore the label, and a jolly man asked her if she was in on their package. 'Gate number 7. Our plane is on time,' he said. He was accompanied by his wife and two teenage daughters. Lydia followed him and a little while later was sitting aboard the aeroplane. Really, there was little to get nervous about. Everybody seemed quite ordinary and, in some ways, it was less trouble than travelling to Bognor Regis. A meal was served on the journey – a large slice of pork pie and salad. This was followed by coffee. Lydia asked for tea, and a cup was produced for her without bother. By the time she had eaten, drunk her tea and read a little of her book, it was announced that they were due to land at Monastir. Lydia felt she had hardly travelled at all, let alone was about to land in North Africa. Apart from the heat and a little less formality by customs officials, the airport seemed to be a smaller version of the one that she had left. It was silly of her, but she was disappointed at not seeing a minaret. For some reason, she had imagined that one would come into view. Her first view of North Africa was a lot of concrete and glass doors.

'Delmar Tour Group this way, please.' A very smart lady wearing a dark green skirt and a pale blue blouse ushered Lydia's group into a corner of the vast reception room at the airport. 'I am your tour leader. My name is Nancy,' she smiled brightly. On her head she wore a strange hat shaped rather like a tea-cosy. It was worn in Napoleonic fashion, and 'Delmar Tours' was embroidered in dark green lettering across the pale blue cloth. Nancy could not be missed.

Another group of people seemed to be returning to England. Some carried mementoes of their holidays. Straw hats, felt camels, a bird-cage, a brass metal tray, were all being trundled into view.

A middle-aged man broke away from this group and appeared to be in some kind of agitation. He approached Lydia's group hurriedly. Beads of perspiration stood out on his brow. He fumbled in his pocket and took out some notes. 'Look, I have some currency here. It's worth £10. I'll let it go for five. I can't take the money out with me, and it's useless in London,' he appealed to the group who remained silent and still. Perhaps it was his distress that embarrassed them. In any event his offer was met with no response.

'Just a minute,' Lydia called after him, and handed him a £5 note. He pressed the bundle of notes into her hand and quickly made his way to the Tunisian customs desk.

'You were taking a risk, you know.' A male fellow-traveller with a Lancashire accent frowned at Lydia when she returned with the money in her hand.

'It's worth over £11,' said Lydia as she counted the notes. 'I won't be able to thank him now.'

'You were taking a risk there.' The man from Lancashire repeated himself, and for a moment Lydia was reminded of Barbara.

'Delmar Tour Group this way, please. Delmar Tour Group this way, please. This way.' Nancy beckoned as she spoke, and thirty or more people followed behind her and she led them from the airport into the mid-day heat outside its precincts. She produced what looked like a register from her briefcase.

'Could you gather round me, please? Yes, as close as you can. When I call out your name, I will give you your coach number.' Six buses were lined up nearby. 'Would you mind answering "Yes, Nancy" before leaving for your coach, and I can tick you off the list. I'll call out your names alphabetically.'

Lydia felt as though she were returning to school. 'P' always came near the end; she placed her case on the ground and sat on it. The heat could make one irritable, and if there was any waiting to be done, it was as to be as comfortable as possible. The names were called out loud and clear: Adams, Allen, Battersby. People began to move and climb aboard the buses. Lydia looked about her. Nancy's voice became more distant, and Lydia surveyed the brown, burnt-out landscape. A glimpse of a palm tree set her imagination in motion. Benny was running behind a tank, taking cover from flying shrapnel as shells burst about him and now, more than thirty years later . . .

'Poulton, Poulton. Is there a Mrs Lydia Poulton? Poulton – was anyone travelling near or has anyone talked to a Mrs Poulton?' Nancy's shrill voice broke Lydia's reverie.

'I'm here. I'm Mrs Poulton,' Lydia called out.

'Coach number 6, Mrs Poulton. Number 6.' Nancy called out the number more loudly than she had done for the others and articulated her words more carefully. Lydia said 'Thank you' and made her way to the coach, convinced that her tour leader thought she was either deaf or slightly retarded. The coach was full, all couples and families. There were no seats to spare. As far as she could see, Lydia was the only person travelling alone.

'Is this coach number 6?' she asked a young woman sitting near the door.

'Yes, dear,' the younger woman replied.

'Well, I was directed to number 6. I'm sure I have the right number . . .'

'*Oui. oui.*' The driver of the bus turned his moustached face towards her and patted a single seat between him and the gear box. 'Here, it is good. Here, here, come, come.'

Lydia settled herself on the seat, set strangely apart from the rest of the company. She didn't mind. Her view was the best one and she didn't want to chat. Another roll-call was made by Nancy before the coach drove off. Lydia thought it a pity that everything was so smoothly planned. A few mishaps often brought a bit of excitement. Everything so far was planned and predictable. The coach started.

'Here, you take. It is good.' The coach driver had taken a sprig of white flowers which somehow had managed to lodge behind his right ear. Lydia sniffed. The perfume was heavy, sweet and quite overwhelming. She held the flowers closer to her nostrils as the coach began its journey. The predictability had been broken and Lydia felt, just slightly, that she was commencing a holiday. Odd that a spray of jasmine could represent so much. It was all a matter of timing, thought Lydia, all a matter of timing.

It was very hot. Lydia wafted the spray of jasmine in front of her face as though it were a windscreen-wiper. The landscape did not impress her. Flat, burnt-out, brown plains stretched on one side of the road. The prickly bushes looked grey, and Lydia wondered whether they were dead or covered in dust. The sea and the occasional palm tree on one side, the burnt-out plain on the other, there was nothing to divert the eye, very little sign of anything living. Occasionally they passed a small shack which might once have been a house. The shacks were derelict, empty. It was almost as though the route had been evacuated. Tourism appeared to have provided its own peculiar brand of warfare. Lydia felt as though she might just as well have been travelling in a tank. She did not resist the drowsiness, the thoughts of Benny. She closed her eyes. The jasmine ceased to flutter and came to rest on her lap. Lydia slept.

The screeching of brakes and the coach bumping to a stop awoke her.

'This is our first drop. I believe over half of you are booked in here. This is the renowned Hotel El Nabeul, first opened in 1974. It is within the same grounds as the Hotel Remada and alongside its sister hotel, El Remana. You will find all you require here. Its facilities include an American Bar, indoor and open-air swimming-pools, a nightly discothèque. Within the spacious dining-room you have a choice of *table d'hôte* menu or running buffet. There is a hairdressing salon, and lifts serve all floors of the modern, comfortable bedrooms.'

Nancy's last piece of information cleared Lydia's head of sleep. It had conjured up her night in the New Forest. She glanced from the window. The hotel was enormous. It curved around to form a semi-circle, a great, white, balconied concrete giant. Lydia thought it looked like a wedding cake cut in half. The grounds were luxurious, green from water-sprayers. She glimpsed a swimming-pool as well as numerous coloured shades dotted around. A few Europeans were to be seen, all in bathing costumes, their skins in various shades of light brown, glistening from endless applications of sun oil. Half the people left the coach as Nancy piped another roll-call. Five other hotels were called at, and Lydia found that her name was not down for the last of these. She remained sitting next to the driver. Nancy had clutched her belongings and was on the point of leaving before she turned as her foot reached the second step of the bus.

'Oh, I'm sorry, Mrs Poulton. Don't worry, I hadn't

forgotten you.' She had, thought Lydia, but smiled as if to say 'I'm not worried.' She wasn't. 'You see, all the modern hotels line the shore to the north of the town. As you can see, their positions are ideal as they overlook the lovely sandy beach. They constitute the northern end of what we term the New Town.'

'It was because of the war,' said Lydia.

'Pardon, dear?' Again Nancy addressed Lydia as if senility had reduced her to a hearing-trumpet. Lydia sniffed her jasmine.

'The part of the town where everything had to be completely rebuilt; it was reduced to rubble during the last war. I had a friend . . .'

'Yes, dear, I see.' Nancy was in a hurry. 'I'm sorry we couldn't fit you in – as a single – at any of the newer hotels. I'm afraid the only place we could find was the Hotel du Sud. It's in the centre of the town. It has its own swimming pool and backs onto the beach. I'm afraid it's almost a mile from here. You won't mind if I don't accompany you? If you want to contact me, you may telephone the Nabeul any morning at eleven. I'm always there. The driver will see you arrive safely.'

Lydia didn't want to talk to Nancy; she would accept whatever turned up. She couldn't be bothered to ask any questions. She smiled and waved her jasmine and Nancy left. Both women felt relieved after the farewell. It was like that when communication lines had been inadvertently broken or never even met.

'It's good, ver' good, better. Tunisian, very good. Hotel du Sud better; *près de medina*, near *medina*. Hotel du Sud. You like. Arab, *très joli*,' the driver answered Lydia and patted her knee – almost slapped it, in fact. Men were often unaware of their own strength, Lydia thought.

His insights or instincts proved correct. There were no private grounds to the frontage of the Hotel du Sud. There were tables on the pavement of the main road. The whole frontage was inundated with tables. There were Tunisians sitting at them. Beyond the road was a railway which ran directly to the harbour. Lydia could see the boats. But more breath-taking was the sight of the ramparts of the old part of the town – the *medina* – which rose up not 500 yards from her hotel.

'Oh,' Lydia cried. The driver pulled the bus to a halt.

'*Medina, medina.*' He smiled and followed her gaze. Lydia stood up to reach for her case from the rack. The driver restrained her, removing her hand from the handle of the case. He took the case and motioned to her that she should follow him.

They climbed four steps which provided a terrace to the frontage of the hotel and formed a viewing platform for the street. Inside the hotel Lydia was welcomed by an attractive young woman who stood behind the reception desk. Three young men, dressed in scarlet uniforms, stood behind the desk. The woman was very busy answering the telephone and presumably checking accounts. The men appeared to be doing nothing – that is, if standing behind the desk could be counted as doing nothing. The woman checked Lydia's name on her lists and asked her to wait for a few moments in the adjacent lounge.

The driver followed her and placed her case near the huge armchair she had settled herself into. She thanked him, in English. He smiled. He had been very kind. Quite aware that she was vastly over-tipping him, Lydia gave him one of the notes she had obtained on her first venture into the exchange rate. After all, she had made a big profit. What had she got to lose? Spread a bit of it around.

The driver stared at her in disbelief, holding it between his fingers. Lydia patted his hand. 'It's all right, I know the value. Please accept it.' He placed the note in his pocket and stood at Lydia's side. She had expected him to leave. She was surprised when, after a few minutes, he left without saying anything. It seemed out of character as far as this particular man was concerned, Tunisian or not. Before she could reflect further on his action he had returned to bring her a glass of cold, crushed orange. He placed the glass at the table and nodded that the service was his pleasure. Lydia accepted the drink gratefully. She had become quite thirsty.

After twenty minutes had gone by, she began to think that she might have been forgotten. She felt hot and sticky.

She felt the need of a shower or a bath and, yes, she had to admit it, the need for a rest. She glanced at her wristwatch. The driver noted her every movement. The glance at her watch seemed to crack him into action like the bang from a starting-pistol.

She could hear his voice from where she was sitting. He was speaking loudly, in Arabic. His voice rose and he had begun to shout. There were some responses, then the exchanges stopped. He returned with two scarlet-uniformed youths. One of them took Lydia's case. The other showed her that he held the keys to her room. The four of them walked back to the reception desk. The driver touched Lydia's shoulder. She shook his hand. He turned to the reception.

'She is lady. Good lady. Mrs Poooolton.' He spoke rapid Arabic, and Lydia wondered whether he were delivering more strictures with regard to her welfare. 'I go now, goodbye. Thank you.'

'Goodbye,' Lydia called after him. She followed the two youths, empty handed apart from the jasmine. The white petals had begun to wither, and some of them had turned brown, yet the fragrance was still as strong as ever.

One of the youths pressed the lift button but nothing happened. He indicated that they should take the stairway. Lydia was relieved to find that her room was situated on a corridor on the first floor. This meant she could forget the lift. She had never liked lifts. Room number 23. The youths were courteous. They showed her the bathroom, the shower, the large balcony, the wardrobe and clothing space, handed her the keys, nodded politely and then left her.

It was a large room. Then Lydia was momentarily astonished. There were two beds. She looked in the ward-robe space that was next to the one she had been shown. Clothes hung from the racks, a woman's clothes. Her eyes noticed an array of cosmetics on one of the two dressing-tables. The coverlet of one of the beds had been folded back to indicate that it was 'booked'. Lydia had not expected to be sharing a room. Perhaps she should complain, but then, what did the other woman feel? She might just as well have been under the same misapprehension as herself. Yet she had apportioned space within the room with meticulous fairness. Lydia unpacked her clothes, took a bath and wound a long pink cotton robe about her plump naked- ness. She stood on the balcony. She could almost touch the palm leaves that dropped from a nearby tree. A small swimming-pool lay beyond and, further on, there was a stretch of sand and then the sea. An iron fence and iron gateway led on to the beach.

Everything seemed most accessible in this hotel. To the front was the real city of Sousse. To the back was the sea. Lydia placed her jasmine in a tumbler of water and lay down on her bed. She tried to think of Benny; of his stay here; of the roaring of aeroplanes and the rattle of machine- gun fire. Somehow she could not sustain the imagery. The occasional plop of someone diving into the pool and the insistent murmuring of the sea convinced her that this was not the same place. She closed her eyes. She did not feel upset, and fell asleep feeling slightly guilty.

14

Lydia awoke. It took her some time before she could remember that she had come out of a slumber and was in North Africa. She had slept heavily and lay still for a while on top of the bed before plumping her two pillows behind her and raising herself into a sitting position.

'Oh, my God, I've woken you up; my first boob.' The voice came from the balcony. 'It's at least an hour and a half before dinner. I can have some tea sent up, but I usually make myself a cocktail around about now. I have my own supply of liquor here. The prices here with regard to liquor just don't bear thinking of. My dear, a multi-millionaire would have to consult an accountant before he even thought of getting tipsy. I don't mean the wine, just the straight stuff. It's all to do with their religion, and import – something like that. Everything else is fine – look, before I go any further, make me a promise. Just tell me to shut up from time to time. I'm a yapper. Yap, yap, yap. It used to be a problem but now I've gotten to learn to live with it, so if I'm yapping, quieten me. Down, Fido, down. That's what my second husband used to say.'

The speaker was a small, thin woman. She stood framed in the balcony doorway, and it was impossible for Lydia to distinguish any more features as the sun behind the woman had transformed them into a silhouette. The silhouette spoke with an American accent.

'I'm Lydia, Lydia Poulton. You didn't wake me.'

'Look, there I go, yapping without introducing myself.' The woman left the balcony and perched herself on the edge of Lydia's bed. She extended a claw-like, be-ringed hand with nails that were painted a bright orange. The two women touched hands lightly. 'I'm Avril, Avril Leary. No, my God, no, I'm Avril Macey. You see, I've been married four times and the second husband (God rest him counted the most, so I still lapse into being Leary when I've been Macey for four years, now. He's gone, too.'

'Who?'

'Oh, Macey; got killed in a çar crash. Yup, two divorces, two deaths, four men; it's not the whole of my life but here I am sixty-three and on my own. I'm alive, though.'

'Nobody could quarrel with that, Avril,' giggled Lydia.

Avril left the bed, went to the bathroom and returned with two tumblers containing a very pale-coloured liquid. She handed Lydia one of the glasses.

'I fixed us a cocktail. I always have one just before dinner. I've been here for three days and, believe me, I've needed this drink. All tables are numbered, and there I am sitting at a table set for two, next to a gorgeous fountain, and I eat alone. Can you imagine it? All the company I've had at meal times has been a fountain and an empty chair.'

'Ugh.' Lydia had taken a sip of her drink.

'I make 'em strong. Just sip it slowly. It's the side effect that counts, not the taste.' Avril held up her glass in a gesture of toasting Lydia and followed her own advice by taking a bird-like sip.

Lydia looked at the woman. Her first impression had been that Avril wore a great deal of make-up. On closer scrutiny she realized that this conclusion was far from the truth. Avril's complexion, a deep golden brown to all intents and purposes, was her own. No traces of powder filled the skin which shone. The places where lines of age are most pronounced were made up, except for the corners of the mouth. Presumably Avril could do nothing about these defined tracks. They curved upwards – which might have meant that she smiled a lot. The lips and eyes were both made up with glitter, an orange lipstick with gold speckles decorated the mouth, and the eyes were large and dark brown. The eyelids, the space between the eye-brow and the crow's nest area of the eyes, were coloured turquoise, speckled once more, but with silver glitter. The hair was cropped short. It was dark brown with blonde streaks bursting here and there. 'A painted sparrow,' thought Lydia. 'All eyes, beak and chirp. Throw a sparrow a few crumbs and . . .'

'I suppose you've been married?' Avril drew her striped towelling robe about her knees.

'Just once.'

Avril was quick to peck at Lydia's unenthusiastic response. 'Any romances?' she asked.

'Yes. One. Just one.' Lydia did not look at Avril as she spoke but pretended to look for somewhere to place her drink.

'He was your Leary?'

'Pardon?'

'You didn't tell me his name, but I can tell. He was the one that counted, wasn't he?'

'Yes.'

'Dead?'

'I'm afraid so, yes.'

'Leary too, but they wouldn't want us to fade into decline, would they? I know they wouldn't. At least, Leary wouldn't want me to.'

'No, Benny wouldn't have wanted me to either.' Lydia had spoken his name and felt relieved.

'All of mine were in the mind business. One psychologist, one psychiatrist and two psychoanalysts.'

Lydia didn't dare ask Avril to explain the differences involved in the working groups mentioned. Avril had made it sound like different kinds of shops. She might as well have said greengrocer, hardware and news-agent. Avril sipped her drink and left a silver speckle on the rim of her glass.

'They're the only groups I've ever been attracted to – I mean to live with. Sexually, two of them ought to have stayed on the couch themselves and never got off it. Perhaps it was my yapping that put them off; it never bothered Leary. You know, I've seen him come in, tired, drained, squeezed out of moisture from listening. I'd tell myself: "Avril, just fix him a drink and leave him alone for an hour or two. Then a quiet salad and steak dinner." But, no, I'd give him the drink and off I'd go, yap, yap, yap. Sometimes he'd fall asleep with me still yapping. Oh, he was so good to me that man. He'd talk in bed sometimes. My God, that was the only place that I gave him the chance.

Boy, oh, boy, when he talked in bed I listened. I think my yapping might have helped cause his brain haemorrhage.' Avril's up-turned mouth drooped.

'Oh, I don't think so, dear. Oh no, certainly not. I think he must have loved listening to you.' Lydia spoke with confidence. Avril, startled by the observation, placed her drink on the small dresser next to the bed.

'Look, Lydia, I prattle on about nothing. Why, I could spend thirty minutes on the morning's weather without taking a breath. What would he be wanting to know about the morning's weather when the morning was over and gone?' Avril gestured her despair by opening the palms of both her hands. She had picked the gesture up from one of her earlier husbands who was Jewish.

'It sounds to me as though you were perfect for him. Given what his job entailed, dear, he must have thought about it before he asked you to marry him.' Avril dropped her hands as Lydia spoke and shook her head from side to side.

'No, I kinda think he was feeling sorry for me. He proposed by telephone. I was freewheeling at the time. I mean, he was divorced and playing the field. He'd been one of the players. There were others. Then one night I got this phone call. "Avril," he said, "You're not getting any younger. I think you should marry me. I'd like it if you would. What d'ya say?" Well, I said yes immediately. "OK," he said. "I'll make the arrangements." He did, too. We were all signed, sealed and legalized in a week. Oh, I was so happy with him. You'd think being content would have made me talk less, but no, I think I prattled more.'

'He must have adored it,' Lydia said.

'What?'

'The prattle. It must have been such a comfort to him. Imagine him with his patients, my dear, listening all day, each day and every day, and listening intently. And then, trying to make some sense or some meaning from the words in order to cure a grief or a wound.' Lydia paused and bit her bottom lip – Henry in the last ten years of her marriage to him had often told her to save her breath when she had begun to recount the mundane events of her day to him.

'Avril, my dear, you must have been heaven-sent, chirping away like some bright bird – a human canary.'

Avril was silent. She frowned. It was not like her to be at a loss for words. She moved closer to Lydia and held her head to one side.

'You're not, you've never been, a psychiatrist, have you?'

'Oh, no dear.'

'I mean, did you train in any of the professions connected with – er – the mind?'

'I've always been a housewife,' said Lydia.

'You had children?'

'Yes, two, a boy and a girl. Both married. I'm a grand-mother to three now.'

Avril sighed as Lydia gave her the family statistics. Her turquoise eyelids fluttered and the orange mouth twitched. 'I always wanted children. I'm Catholic, you know. Lapsed, badly lapsed. I lapsed when I was twenty and, believe me, it wasn't fashionable then.'

'What?'

'Lapsing. My first husband was a psychiatrist. He had just finished in training when I met him. He was a thin man, with a handsome but sensitive face. It ended there – his sensitivity, I mean. You won't believe this but he actually talked me into bed with him.' (Lydia did, indeed, find this hard to believe but chose not to interrupt.) 'I would let him go so far and then I'd stop the canoodling when it began to get out of hand. Don't get me wrong: I wanted it to get out of hand but not before I had that gold ring on my finger. He didn't seem to understand. I explained that it was part of my faith, even when he was trying to pull my knickers off and I was trying to keep them on. After about four months together, he told me that I was sick and until I got myself cured he'd stop seeing me.'

'What was wrong with you, my dear?'

'Nothing physical – at least, I didn't think it was, but he was convinced. He said I was suffering from some special type of frigidity. Well, I'd always thought of myself as a rather warm, out-going person. He kept his word. He

never contacted me for over a month. Not even a telephone
call. You know how it is when you feel that way about a
man. I waited for that telephone call each night, just like
they say women do on pop records and some films. I
believed he might be right, after a while – so I telephoned
him. He answered me and said, "I'm looking for a cure for
you tonight, sugar."'

'I don't think he sounds very nice,' said Lydia.

'Was your first one nice?'

'Not very. No, not very,' Lydia answered grudgingly.
She hated to be disloyal.

'How would I know whether he was nice or not? He came
round that night. He said he had to stay the night. I agreed.
"Relax, relax," he kept telling me. In the morning he said I
needed more training. All I did was to go straight to a priest
and then afterwards pray I hadn't got pregnant. Oh, that
was another thing. He said contraception would break the
rhythm. I couldn't bring myself to get any kind of contraception and he was too concerned with his rhythm.
During the six months that followed, all I did was pray after
the nights that he stayed over. It never happened. I never
did get pregnant. When he proposed to me, he said I'd
make a good receptionist. He'd struck out private. Well, we
married and I worked for him. Unpaid, I might add. I didn't
mind. I wasn't having to go through the same damned
prayer every morning. We did well. He was a good
businessman, and he sure knew how to help people relax.
After a couple of years or so, tax-wise he was better off
employing a secretary/receptionist rather than me. I was
happy to be at home. He had gotten a bigger place and there
was plenty to do.

'Then, one day, he said: "Avril, I guess you can take it out
now." I thought he was referring to his steak – he always
liked it well done, and I'd only just placed it under the grill.
"It'll be full of blood," I said. "For Christ sake, don't be so
fucking medieval. Any hospital will do the job in five
minutes. There's no mess to it. Women have coils removed
every day." Then he smiled, "I'd like a baby. We can afford
one now. Make an appointment to get the coil out."' Avril
shook her head.

'There never was a coil in. I went to the hospital. Verdict – hopeless. Fallopian problems. I was barren. I could go on relaxing for ever. I won the divorce. Another receptionist has borne him four children. I guess she never prayed. You don't want to go through all of them?'

'What?'

'My husbands. No, for God's sake, I've broken my resolutions already – but you're such a good listener. Is the drink a bit strong for you?' Avril had noticed Lydia's nose wrinkle as she sipped.

'Yes, it is a bit strong – I don't think I'll be able to drink it all before dinner. My head tends to spin.' Lydia put her hand to her brow.

'I'll shut up. Would you like a little music?' Avril spoke almost apologetically. She needn't have. Lydia had already decided she liked her.

'Yes, a song. You choose one.' Lydia could see that Avril had three cassettes near her bed.

'It came out in 1964. It seems a long while ago. The Beatles, "I Want To Hold Your Hand".' Lydia listened. She remembered it.

'Play it again, Avril. Let's dance and twirl about a bit, shall we?' Lydia had already begun to sway and the two strangers held hands to the music.

They descended the steps to the dining-room with arms linked, both 'dressed' for the occasion. Avril had gone native and wore a scarlet ankle-length shift, whilst Lydia wore a silk flower-patterned dress whose edges also touched the stairs as she placed one foot before the other.

'Now that we know we like one another, I have a confession,' said Avril.

'I'm not a priest, dear.' Lydia thought they might be about to embark on another husband.

'I guess I should have told you first thing. We're entitled to a £60 rebate from the management.'

'What?' Lydia paused on the stairway. Avril looked guilty.

'It's because we've agreed to share the room. I hadn't mentioned it because, if I hadn't liked you, they could have stuck their £60 up their . . .'

'Yes, I was booked for a single,' said Lydia.

'Look, if I'm too much, say so; there's no hard feelings. I know how . . .'

'Avril, please stop. I was really thinking how lucky I was being able to share with you. Now you announce a £60 bonus. I'd have shared with or without the money, but now it's come our way I think we should spend it, don't you?'

'Sure, sure, we'll have a ball. Let's hit the town. We've nothing to lose.' Avril was happy.

'Nothing to lose.' Lydia reiterated the words as the fountain came into view.

All the waiters were young. An older hierarchy of four men between thirty-five and forty-five years of age directed operations whilst the younger men made their ways between the dining-tables. The young waiters were smartly dressed, efficient, courteous and yet Avril was trying to think why or what was different about them from waiters she had observed in other countries. She cogitated over this, whilst Lydia glanced about her to absorb her surroundings in more detail. Avril snapped her fingers quite loudly. This startled Lydia and caused her to spill a little wine on the table.

'Oh, I do wish you wouldn't do that, dear.' Lydia dabbed the wine with her napkin and watched the red stain spread on the tablecloth like a map with uncontrollable contours.

'Oh, my God, Lydia, I'm sorry but the dawn has broken. I know how this lot are different.'

'Which lot?' Lydia was still feeling a little cross about the spilt wine.

'The waiters.'

'They seem perfect to me. All very good-looking, too. In their early twenties, most of them seem to be, but I'm hopeless about age. I can't see . . .'

'It's the way they move,' said Avril as though she had just sighted Niagara Falls. 'Waiters in other countries glide. They bend and weave between the tables. Their bodies sway this way and that, a little like dancers; but these, these move like football players. Perhaps it's their hips that just stay in one place.'

'They can be balletic, too. Footballers can be most grace-
ful, but as regards the waiters I think I understand what you
mean.' Lydia was pleased that Avril's veal cutlet had arrived. As her friend chewed, Lydia took the opportunity to
enjoy her surroundings without being diverted by the
international analysis of waiters' walking habits. 'Poor
men, always dressed to look like penguins,' thought Lydia.

Lydia was tempted to stretch out her arm and let the
waters of the fountain which cascaded and fell not a metre
away from their table touch her hand. The fountain, and
the pool that it fed, was the centre-piece of the dining-
room. All the tables were dotted about around it with an *ad
hoc*-ism that Lydia found pleasing. Each table was numbered but Lydia had the pleasant feeling that the waiters
had a mental registration of the people that they served
rather than the table number. The thought pleased her. She
moved her chair to the edge of the pool. Fish swam about in
it. They moved slowly as if they were drugged. There was
no darting about or quick change of direction. They were
large fish, dreamy creatures.

Near the edge of the pool Lydia was disappointed to see
what could only be a plastic lobster. It was bright blue in
colour, dotted with white spots. Its claws were large and
rather badly constructed. They almost seemed deformed.
Perhaps some child had discarded it, or a tourist might have
thought it would aesthetically improve the barren, marble
bed.

Conscious of the fact that she was behaving somewhat
daringly, Lydia clutched the edge of the fountain with one
hand and slowly plunged her other hand, wrist and fore-
arm into the water. It was deeper than it seemed. She leaned
further over, her left arm now strung out taut as a wire, as it
held her from entering the pool bodily. The water was well
past her right elbow before she could grasp the bright blue
object. She managed to get four fingers around the region
of its head. The great claw, the large, deformed-looking
one, reared up and snapped at her plump fingers. The
creature swivelled, ready for an attack. The fingers must
have looked like a small squid to him – why should he not
be irritated by the intrusion? Lydia's shock soon turned to

abject horror as she realized that she would not be able to haul herself back into position in time without hazarding falling into the pool. The claw opened. Lydia half-screamed, released her grasp on the fountain's edge and, in the half-moment as she fell towards the water, hoped she was dreaming.

One hand was on her left shoulder and the other was cupped under her left breast. She was not in the water. Still dazed, she watched the creature scuttle not more than a few inches. Then it became static, its feelers immobile, a plastic impostor once more. The young waiter still held her. 'I'm all right, now, thank you.' He removed his hands from her. Regality had never been one of her attributes but she attempted to return to her table as though nothing had happened. The waiter slipped the chair expertly beneath her behind as she rejoined Avril.

'*Langouste?* You like *langouste*?' He was a tactful waiter but could not suppress the grin which spread across his face.

'That means lobster, dear,' said Avril, whose veal had almost gone cold because of the somewhat vicarious pleasure she had taken in watching Lydia's antics.

Lydia turned to the waiter. 'Not alive, no. I don't like them alive.' The waiter's vocabulary was limited to the bare essentials of table service. For response, all he could do was smile. He placed Lydia's main course before her. It was grilled fish. The head and tail remained intact. Lydia looked at it, and paused. 'It's not from the pool, is it?' She pointed to the fountain. He shook his head.

'*Non, non*, no, *nein*, *pour*, *pour*, for . . .'

'Decoration,' said Avril, supportive to the last.

'From the sea.' He pointed to the fish. Aware that his English had expanded, he repeated the phrase. 'From the sea.' Lydia knew she was being childish, but was grateful for the information.

'Mrs Poolton, Mrs Macey.' He nodded to them both, then placed his hand on his chest, somewhere in the region of his heart. 'Ahmed.' He poured their first glass of wine. He was neither over-attentive nor perfunctory. His introduction left the elderly ladies quite moved. It was Lydia who spoke first. Avril's unfinished cutlet could not be left any longer without becoming entirely inedible.

'Yes, these waiters are different.' Lydia sliced the head and tail off her fish. 'I hope they give them lots of time for football. Football with a large pitch, and a referee that was not too harsh. Yes, I would hope for a lot of space for them, green space and lots of time, time to be wild . . . and free – no constrictions of dress and formality. Perhaps they ought to be allowed to play naked in the sun and . . .'

Avril interrupted her. 'Lydia, did anyone ever tell you you were romantic?' She topped up Lydia's glass as she spoke.

'No,' Lydia answered her quietly.

'Mrs Pooolton, Mrs Pooolton.' Avril raised her glass.

'Mrs Macey.' Lydia held up her glass.

The two women savoured the moment before they drank. Friendship was like that, thought Lydia. It either emerged slowly and then, quite suddenly, was there. Or, as with middle-age, it popped up like a mushroom. Where has the rest of my life gone? And where were you whilst it was going?

15

It was the early morning of the fourth day the two women had spent together. They sat on the balcony of their room, enjoying the silence, the air and each other's company. They had ordered tea to be delivered to their room but it was still only 7 a.m. The tea would arrive around 7.30. The half-hour wait did not concern them. Within the period of time they had spent together they had both gleaned that a planned day meant a dependence on punctuality, which neither sought. So they sat, as though meditating under the dictatorship of some revered guru. However, their minds were not empty.

If it had been possible to ram the two ladies down a computer, it would have been unlikely that the machine would have found them at all compatible. Given the data available, it might even have broken down in its processing. Logically they seemed an impossible pair. Looking at it in nationalistic terms, if someone had commissioned an artist to design a single flag which combined the Union Jack with the Stars and Stripes – and improve the design of both flags in one single pattern – any self-respecting artist would reject the proposition as being impossible.

The two women had influenced and improved one another even to the extent of appearance. Avril had shed a little of her gilt and glitter, and Lydia had gained some of it. Avril looked less vulgar and Lydia less frumpish.

The sun and salt sea-spray had quickly reduced Lydia's soft perm to a dry, brittle mass of tight curls which sprouted from her head like pieces of coiled silver wire. Avril had applied conditioner to it, but within an hour it reverted to its former resistant position. It was after two of Avril's special martinis that Lydia had agreed to let Avril cut her hair. The snipping and snapping of the scissors had seemed to go on for quite an unaccountably long time, and Lydia, whose half-drunken stupor had begun to wane, was seriously considering the possibilities of wearing a wig if she were to emerge entirely bald from the onslaught. Her fears had been groundless. Lydia had imagined that urchin cuts were for teenagers, but on viewing the soft wisps of hair which now framed her brow and ears, she was more than pleasantly surprised.

'There, just look and see how much softer it makes your face look.' Avril had stood back from her handiwork and looked over Lydia's shoulder as they viewed the transformation in the mirror. 'Why have your hair cooked each week? Hair was never meant for cooking. All you need to do now is shampoo it, pin it occasionally, and brush it. A light blue rinse might help . . .' Avril had been most matter-of-fact.

In the short walks they had taken together, Avril had chosen to wear enormous sun glasses which fitted completely about her eyes. Lydia had never seen such ugly spectacles – indeed, to all intents and purposes they resembled underwater diving-goggles. At thirty-minute intervals it was necessary for Avril to pause and apply eye drops in spite of the heavy protection she wore about her eyes.

'I'm allergic to dust. My eyes are so sensitive,' she had said as Lydia had administered some drops to her left eye one afternoon as they sat at a café table. Lydia was sure that no dust could ever penetrate the goggles and, there, that afternoon, she could see the tiny speckles of silver enmeshed in Avril's eyeball. The next day Avril had the joy of leaving her goggles behind: the speckled eye shadow had been dropped into the waste-paper bin. Lydia's light blue shadow flecked Avril's eye-lids one day, and Avril purchased a light green shadow to ring the changes for another. Her eyes, which were an attractive dark brown, could now be seen, and her vision greatly improved. Dust affected her no more and no less than anyone else. She squinted less, and the lines at the corners of her eyes had become distinctly less pronounced.

As far as dress was concerned, both women had opted for comfort. Each had purchased the simple shifts that some liberated Tunisian women wore. They were cool, comfortable and as flattering to the ample figure as to the scraggy one. Size was no problem. For Lydia, getting dressed each day was a most simple process. All she wore was knickers, bra and then the shift. Avril's adornment was even more sparse. Her breasts needed no bra, and at times she had confessed to Lydia that she had forgotten to put on any knickers. Neither of the women enjoyed lying exposed and oiled, sacrificed to the sun like ancient Incas in somnambulant worship of the rays. This was what most of the tourists wished, and many of them never left the immediate environs of the hotel swimming-pool and the beach except to eat. Avril had bought bottles of lotion which achieved a tan without any form of pagan worship. A liberal application once every two days had given both women the faint golden glow they required. In particular, Lydia's veins looked less stark against a gold background than they had against a white one.

'Oh, there was a telephone message for you from your courier.' Avril spoke to Lydia as the two women were leaving the hotel. 'If you want to take a trip to Carthage, you are to contact her or leave a message for her before eleven this morning.' Avril glanced at her watch. 'It's 10.30 now, so if you . . .'

Lydia shook her head. 'No, I don't want to make any plans. It's nice just taking things day by day.'

They stepped into the late morning sunlight. They had decided to purchase two more shifts each. This meant that they would have five each. The garments washed easily and dried quickly. Without too much effort they could achieve a change of wardrobe twice a day. This was their third sortie into the *medina*. On their first expedition they had been subject to a lot of over-attention, curiosity and, if one wished to look at things puritanically, harassment.

There seemed to be a surplus of young men about the town who wished to be helpful. Did the ladies require a guide? Were the ladies alone? Had the ladies seen the catacombs? Were the ladies Swedish, German, French? If one question thwarted introduction, another was proffered. Were the ladies married?

'My God, what d'you think they think we are, Lydia? Faded actresses or something like that?'

A note of exasperation had crept into Avril's voice after two young men they thought had finally left them positioned themselves not five yards from them as the two ladies sat down at a café table to drink a cold citron. There was a lot to look at, apart from the men. Much as Lydia denied this inner need to look in their direction, she found herself gazing directly at the young men. They stood there nonchalantly smiling, but there was no arrogance in the smiles with which the handsome young men in Europe were so often affected.

Lydia looked at them intently. From what she observed she ought to have been either embarrassed or excited. She felt neither. Hands in pockets, they gently caressed their genitals. Lydia had noticed that many of the men in this age group did this, so that she was not at all surprised to see that both men now in her view were in a semi or full state of erection. She wondered whether they were wholly conscious of this fact.

'My God, d'you see what they're doing?' Avril had followed Lydia's stare.

'I think it has something to do with the climate,' Lydia had said and had diverted Avril's worried gaze to a small child, not more than a few years of age, who was attempting to sell a sheepskin rug almost twice his own size. The child had been more insistent on selling his commodity than the men, and eventually the two women gave him some small change in order that he should leave them alone and take his goods elsewhere. The two men had done likewise and now sat talking happily with two German tourists who had cameras slung about their necks.

After these initial journeys it was as though some bush telegraph had got about the town, and Lydia and Avril still had attendance danced upon them in various ways – but by and large they were not harassed. They chose not to invite it. Each day they visited the *medina*. Its streets and strange alleyways were intricate but, whereas the place was always busy, it was not too large. Both women familiarized themselves with its geography and were in no fear of getting lost within its compounds. They needed no guides. They browsed around comfortably without fear or anxiety. The occasional putrid smell they ignored; there was a lot to hear and so much to see.

'He promised us half price if we bought another one.' Avril was referring to the shifts. They had kept loyally to the same vendor, who now greeted both of them as though they were long-exiled relatives. 'We turn here; then there is that corner where all the herbs are; then the street we want is to the left . . .' Avril talked the directions to herself. She knew that Lydia was paying attention to her.

'Yes, he'll keep it.'

'What's that, Lydia?'

'The man who sells us the shifts. He'll keep his promise if we insist.'

'Ya think so?'

'Oh, I'm sure, dear.' Lydia paused at the corner to look at the array of strange-looking herbs and the woman who was selling them. 'She's probably no older than me,' thought Lydia. This woman cajoled no one to buy her wares. The herbs and spices were wrapped in tiny bundles of paper and handed mutely to the buyers, who always knew exactly what they wanted.

'It would be nice to take little bits of all of this home – but really, I wouldn't know whether to put it in a cake, or flavour the mutton.' Lydia did not really mean what she said. She just felt she would like to make some form of contact with the silent woman who had probably sat with her herbs and spices on this very corner for the past two decades.

'Oh, look, buy some of that orange-looking powder and then – then just use your instinct. I'll get some of those shrivelled roots. They may be ginger. I just love the smell of it.' Avril had already taken some money from her purse. Lydia emulated her friend. Both women touched hands with the sitting lady who sold them a packet of conjecture.

This was the way Lydia and Avril tended to operate. They were sensitive to each other's needs and often cloaked the help they offered one another under the guises with which other people in the past had labelled them. Lydia pretended to be vague and Avril pretended to be brash. Neither woman fooled the other, but they kept up appearances, realizing full well that they were, in all senses, complementary to one another, as well as protective.

'I felt we ought to make some contact with her. She's looked at us each day as we have passed by. It would have been silly just to say "good morning" or "good afternoon" to her, wouldn't it?' Lydia referred to the seed lady as they approached the shift shop.

'Yes, I felt the same myself.' Avril sniffed at the packet of shrivelled roots. 'Lydia, I don't think this is ginger. I'll ask Ahmed at the hotel. Remind me, would you? We should use the stuff now we've bought it, although we could keep it as a souvenir; place it in a bowl and think of the lady sitting there, of the *medina*. Yes, it would evoke everything much better than a snapshot, or maybe one could collect . . .'

The owner of the shift shop had seen them coming and had left the entrance of his store to greet them. He was a small man. Avril (who was not of Amazonian proportions) was a good two inches taller. Throughout the banter Lydia had reason to look down on him in order to view his face. Like the good salesman he purported to be, he apportioned his attention between the women as he escorted them to his shop. This meant that over a stretch of twenty yards he had completely encircled the ladies more than six times. He glided about the two of them, reconnoitering like a friendly Red Indian. If he had been on a pony, the women might have found the short journey less taxing. As it was, before Lydia could answer one of his friendly remarks or questions he had flitted around like some hypnotized gnat and was speaking into Avril's ear. Avril could not begin a sentence before he had left her side to buzz behind her to join Lydia. On reaching the shop, both women felt dizzy.

'Holy Mary, I feel as though I've just stepped off a carousel!' Avril's voice expressed the relief that Lydia felt as the man beckoned them into his store.

'Come, come, please come.' It was more of a gentle order than a request.

His assistant, a boy of thirteen, ushered them beyond the

bales of cloth and neatly stacked djolabas and shifts. He led them beyond the small shop which bulged with merchandise. Only by meticulous tidiness and care bordering on life or death could so much stock have been absorbed and stacked in such a small space. It was miraculous that the vendor could put a hand on any request without too much of a search. The cheapest merchandise was returned to its correct position with the concentration given to some precious jewel. The room beyond provided a stark contrast with the shop itself. White, bare walls, a carpeted floor, four large decorative cushions, three or four folded blankets, a narrow divan couch and a round table gave it the appearance of comfort – but stark comfort. It was as though the owner had maintained the sense of order in his shop but found it necessary to keep his domestic environment as simple as possible. The effect of the room was both peaceful and pleasing. The two women hovered about the entrance.

'Sit, sit, please.' He pointed to the cushions and spoke rapidly in Arabic to the boy. The boy left the room, and Lydia and Avril each sank into a cushion. The little salesman rubbed his hands and smiled a greeting to his guests. He chose to sit on the divan. From his position, he could look down on the two women.

'I hope you like my home, do you?'

The small man spoke good English with a trace of an American accent. Avril had said he had picked up the burr in his voice from seeing American movies. The cinema was very popular with the local populace. Lydia had not disagreed with Avril, but they had gone to the cinema one evening to see *The Guns of Navarone*. Avril was travelling to Rhodes after North Africa, and she thought that a glance at the landscape of Crete might whet her appetite. It was as well that the two women went to view the landscape, as the film had been dubbed in Arabic and the predominantly male audience was rather noisy. In fact, they had not seemed interested in the imposed dialogue and talked through most of it. They cheered through the action sections, and a babble could still be heard when the great gun crashed and exploded. There was no hint of American voices, and the mouths of the players moved at odds with the harsh-sounding voices which had been stamped over them. Lydia decided it was not worth correcting Avril on whether or not the man's accent had been affected by going to the cinema.

The boy entered with a tray of coffee and some small sticky cakes.

'Oh, your home.' Lydia felt she had been remiss in not answering earlier.

'I think this room is charming, yes, charming,' said Avril as she watched the man pour out their coffee as though he were about to serve it from an altar. It was then that Lydia realized that this room *was* his home. The four walls, the blankets, the cushions, the divan were the entirety of his environment. He must eat at one of the *medina* cafés – but where had the coffee come from? Perhaps he shared a kitchen? This small town was full of domestic mysteries which Lydia could not fathom or solve. She added to Avril's appraisal.

'Yes, we do like your home. It's very comfortable, very cosy.'

'Cosy? What is cosy?' Tunisians never let the opportunity of learning something new pass them by. Education, in whatever circumstance it was presented, was grabbed at.

'Cosy is – er, cosy is – er . . .' Avril stretched out her fingers as though she were gesticulating and searching for the explanation. These were measured histrionics as she knew exactly the polite definition that she was about to bestow. 'Cosy is comfortable, attractive, good and small – like you.' She pointed her finger at him, and all three laughed at her pleasantly.

'You have children?' His question was directed to both women. Avril shook her head and Lydia held up two fingers as she was unable to answer because at that moment she had the coffee cup to her mouth.

'Husband?'

'Four,' said Avril.

'Two.' Lydia did not want to be entirely outpaced. The small man's dark eyes widened, and his off-white complexion expressed a genuine surprise.

'Is that possible? Here, a man may take more than one wife, but more than one wife means more children, more trouble. Most men only take one wife. A wife does not take more than one husband. Me, I am not married. I am *celibatère.*'

'Yeah, well, it suits some people, suits me at the moment,' said Avril, who felt that it would be a mistake to commiserate with the man over his bachelorhood. She smiled at him. If he had been just a little smaller, he could almost have been a midget. She supposed that this was the reason he had not married and felt sorry for him.

'Your husbands are here? You make a trip together?'

'No, they are dead,' Lydia answered at once.

'Or gone,' said Avril.

'How old are you?'

'We are adult.' Avril had often encountered the question and always gave the same answer. Lydia felt the need to express it more gently.

'We are as old as we feel. Sometimes we are forty. Sometimes we are 120 and sometimes we are twelve years of age.'

'Lydia, that was beautiful, just beautiful,' said Avril, who was easily moved.

'Me, I am forty-six years. I am alone.' As far as the man was concerned, he had not understood Lydia's reply. He had answered his question to them with an honesty and clarity which jolted both women from the cocoon of defences they chose to set about one another. Avril bit her bottom lip.

'We're alone, too.' Her comment did not satisfy her. It made her feel like a female version of John Wayne, and she had never found him attractive.

Details of London, details of San Franciso and the last drops of coffee had been well and truly drained. Sensing that the two women now wished the visit to be ended, with suitable exchanges, the small man rose from his couch and collected four shifts from the shop. He knew the sizes. His eyes in such matters were detailed and expert. Both Lydia and Avril (from previous personal experience) trusted him implicitly on these matters. It was just a question of colour.

Here again, his instincts had proved that he could appreciate and appraise the taste of his customers. Avril chose one
that was emerald green and Lydia took one of the outsize
ones – deep scarlet: she found the colour dramatic as well as
conservative. They held the shifts close to their bodies,
faced each other, complimented one another, then turned
to the man who stood holding the other two garments they
had chosen not to take. He held one garment over each
arm. They hung from his arms and his short legs and waist.
Lydia and Avril both grinned as he looked as though he
were wearing a lemon and blue two-toned skirt that was
much too long for him. He grinned back.

He held out both arms, like great pennants. The shifts
dropped down from them. His torso and legs were re-
vealed. Both women stopped grinning.

'Oh, hell, we've been misinterpreted.'

Avril stared and frowned. Lydia did not want to hurt the
man's pride. She was not fascinated but was surprised at
the size of his member which stood out from him, large
and erect. One wouldn't have expected such a little man
to be blessed in such a way, yet its size did seem at odds
with his appearance. She was reminded of the lobster's
claw.

'It's very nice, dear, very nice, but put it away now. Very
nice, but put it back in your trousers.' He obeyed her and
accepted her compliment in the generous spirit in which it
was offered; he had always been obliging, and this incident
did not prove to be any exception. Customers' wishes
always came first.

'I guess he was proud of it and just wanted us to take a
peek,' said Avril as she carried both packages under her
arm.

Lydia had developed a blister on her heel and was having
to pick her way with extra care along the cobbled street.

'What, dear?'

'Oh, Lydia, you know, you don't want me to spell it out
for you, do you?'

'Ah, yes, I'd forgotten about that. Yes, dear, I'm sure he
wasn't meaning to upset us or be rude. He wasn't that sort
of man. I don't suppose he has the opportunity to let people

know that it is disproportionate. Although someone ought to tell him that it isn't really important.'

'What?'

'Size.'

'Yeah, I guess technique and timing count for most.'

Avril ruminated and walked on slightly ahead of Lydia, who limped as gracefully as a woman of her size could. The seed lady waved to them and pointed to Lydia's foot; Lydia showed the woman the grey blister which had ballooned on her heel. The woman took Lydia's foot in both hands and deftly unleashed the strap on Lydia's sandal. 'Eh, eh, eh.' She pointed to the other sandal. Lydia took that off herself. The woman took the sandals from the ground and handed them to Lydia.

Walking barefoot was not without hazard. Infections could be picked up. Lydia preferred hazard and freedom. The blister no longer troubled her, and Avril wondered whether or not her friend was just plain dumb, beat or aristocratic. Either way it made no difference – she had come to adore being with the woman.

16

'It's no good blaming Ahmed. You thought up this game. Who are we this week?'

'Are you complaining, honey?'

Avril admired Lydia's heavy, wrought-silver necklace which glimmered slightly as her friend spoke. They had sat down for dinner early, but word seemed to have got around that the two of them were in the dining-room, and the place had quickly begun to fill up. The hotel guests nodded to the two ladies in their bright plumage, as if paying some sort of homage. Avril waved a bangled wrist and Lydia nodded a gracious acknowledgement. The two ladies had become a centre-piece of interest for all the residents of the hotel who had been packaged for their holiday. They could tell their friends in all the semi-detached suburbs of Europe of the two famous and florid ladies who had graced the Hotel du Sud whilst they were there.

Ahmed in all innocence had begun the myth. They tipped him over-generously, they ordered an extra bottle of wine and then, with careless abandon, left over half of its content and requested that it should be given to someone else. He had become very proud of his 'ladies' and had boasted of their fame and generosity in terms of money as well as outlook. When two elderly Frenchmen had requested that the two sisters join them in an aperitif, neither Lydia nor Avril had declared that the bond between them was not genetic. If they were to be cast as sisters, then sisters they would be. It required less explanation.

One of the Frenchmen was a part-time interior decorator, the other a chiropodist. They had lived happily together for years. They had mixed with the best of Parisian society and could recognize class when they saw it. Lydia and Avril spent twenty-five minutes with them. Most of this period was taken up with intermittent showers of admiration and compliments from their French counterparts. The dialogue was in French, and Lydia and Avril understood little of it. They smiled as the phrases tippled forth upon them. The Frenchmen had returned to Paris in the second week. They had been the most appreciative of residents – and had informed the management how fortunate they were in having two such famous ladies staying at the hotel. Ahmed had never doubted their fame. But Lydia and Avril, due to circumstances entirely beyond their control, were forced to consider where their past fame had lain. Actresses seemed the simplest – and that's what they had become.

Avril had said that if they could convince anyone that they were sisters and had been actresses, then, if anyone could be persuaded to swallow two such huge pills of imagination, they *should* have been related and *should* have been actresses. Lydia agreed. Much to her surprise, the pills had been swallowed.

'Oh, dear, this couple are English. It might be more difficult,' said Lydia as she watched a young couple weave their way through the tables in order to approach the table near the fountain.

'How do you know they're English?' Avril eyed the couple.

'He has burnt fore-arms, tried to tan too quickly.'

Both the man and his wife also had red faces. It was as though they were permanently blushing. Only a certain kind of English person could possibly ignore all the warnings in the brochures (as well as the strictures from Nancy) and completely disregard the hottest hours of the day. Lydia did hope that the couple's skin would not peel. Perhaps she should mention how deceptive the sea breezes could be. The breezes were cooling but they did not act as a filter for the hot sun. But a gradual approach to anything was not in the Mumbrys' nature.

'George Mumbry, my wife Angela.' The man thrust his arm forward towards Lydia. His wife attempted to do the same with Avril. Their hands crossed.

'Oh, it's just like New Year's Eve,' said Lydia.

'We are very pleased to meet you both.' Angela eyed one woman, then the other, then looked towards her husband for a meaningful lead into their projected interrogation.

'I am Lydia. This is Avril.' Lydia was now reassured that the couple had come to their table out of a mean kind of curiosity she had always found peculiar to policemen.

'Hi,' said Avril, who had quickly sensed that this couple would be as difficult as Lydia had predicted they would be. She let Angela's hand drop from her own quickly, limply withdrawing her fingers as if they were arthritic and incapable of strength.

'Lovely rings you have,' Angela commented on Avril's hand, which she had left suspended in the air as though her wrist were broken.

'Did you begin your careers in England?' This question came from George.

'You're not at all alike. Are you really sisters?' This question came from Angela.

Lydia patted her wisps of hair. Clearly the niceties of introduction were over. She held up her hand in mild protest.

'One at a time, please! Do you remember the small part you had as a bus-conductress in one of those Ealing comedy films, dear? That was before we left for the States.'

Avril took her cue and laughed accordingly. 'Oh yes, we were both scraggy in those days – weren't you a tea lady in the same film?'

'I don't suppose you could possibly remember any of the Ealing comedy films. No, it would be quite unfair to think you could. You're both much too young to have seen any of them. There are so few films made about the English, now. If we were to rely on the cinema for our national presentation – I mean, of how we are – we would hardly exist, would we? I mean, as far as the rest of the world is concerned!' Avril listened to Lydia's sidetracking with awe.

'That's why we're forced to leave England. It was a terrible wrench. A life as an actress, you might think, is dotted with areas of unemployment. But that was never the case with Avril and me.' Lydia continued, taking just a short pause for breath.

'My God, she's not going to give them a chance to ask any more questions at this rate.' Avril felt suddenly composed.

She knew the strategy. It was 'yap'. Lydia must have learned it from her.

'I think they show an odd one on television now and again, but I can't . . .'

'Television,' Lydia interrupted George and sighed heavily. 'My dears, we've done everything, you know. Our Equity ticket didn't pop out from years at a drama convent. Oh no, we were on the boards at fourteen. Yes, we were two of the original 'Letty Pepp Babes''. We played pantomime in Leeds, Birmingham, Bristol and then there was little time to stop tapping because we were always booked for lengthy summer seasons. The summers seemed longer in England then and, of course, there were more people at the resorts. You know, you wouldn't believe this but we once played an end-of-pier theatre for five months. The show was so good that the locals themselves kept it running till mid-October. Nowadays, you haven't got many piers left, let alone theatres, have you? Then, off we went into pantomime. As we got older we developed our own speciality act.'

'Oh?' George Mumbry wanted to get back to his own table. He was feeling hungry, but he just couldn't get up and leave without appearing rude, and the old dear seemed anxious to go on with much more information than he required or was interested in.

'*Jack and the Beanstalk* gave us a lucrative five years. Of course, we had worked out our own speciality act by then.'

'Did your parents accompany you?' Angela jumped in quickly whilst Lydia drew in some air.

'We're orphans,' said Avril, who was pleased that she had been allowed to make some contribution towards their careers.

'We've always had to be mother and father to one another, dear. That's why we are so close. Although, I must say, it was too close for comfort during the *Jack and the Beanstalk* period.'

'You quarrelled?' asked Angela hopefully.

'Oh, no, dear. It was impossible for us to quarrel. You see, we were the "speciality act" in the show. There is only one cow in that show, but it's most important to the story and rarely off stage in the first act. We made the costume ourselves but it took the two of us to wear it. Avril was the front part. She has always been a little more agile than me. And I was the back. We were in great demand as a cow. Then there was ENSA.'

'War-time performers.' George did not wish to show his ignorance with regard to history but hoped Lydia would not embark on her experiences with Vera Lynn or Bob Hope.

'After the war, the theatre in England had reached a terrible state of decline. The provinces were full of nude shows, naked girls and two comedians thrown in between.'

'Did they have nude shows then?' Angela asked triumphantly. 'Surely they couldn't have done.'

'They certainly did, dear, and precious few people came to the theatres to see them. As I've said, Avril and me have always worked and have always taken what has come along. Nude shows were all that did come along, in those days. Of course, we weren't allowed to move, and stars had to be stuck over our nipples. Both of us went down with pneumonia after one such show which ran to empty houses in a theatre in Darlington. It must have been the draughts. Lots of girls caught flu. We were never compensated. The conditions were terrible.'

'Well, you've weathered that storm pretty well.' George Mumbry had got to his feet, ready to nod a farewell of acknowledgement and defeat.

'Don't ya want to hear about the States?' Avril was ready with a string of epic Westerns she and Lydia had taken part in. Frontier women carrying hoes and chopping logs but always wearing a clean apron, wives of cavalry officers sitting silent and demure, saloon bar molls . . .

'Excuse me, please.' Ahmed placed the evening's menu in Lydia's hands.

'It has been so nice talking to you,' said Angela who had barely spoken a word.

'We'll look for you on the TV when we get back. They do revive things from time to time,' said George, taking his wife's arm.

'Then you're bound to see us. We often pop up here and

there, just a glimpse. I'm sure you'll recognize us,' said Lydia. She half-waved her hand as the couple departed. 'I don't think we'll be troubled by those two again, dear.'

'Pity. I wanted to talk about Hollywood,' said Avril.

Lydia did feel a bit guilty about the way she had commandeered the interview. 'They were always much too large for stars, anyway.'

'Ya what?' Avril noticed that Lydia was dreaming again.

'My nipples.'

'Nipples? What is nipples?' Ahmed frowned and asked Lydia to point them out on the menu.

'How did you know all that stuff, Lydia? The "Know Your City" class couldn't have covered all that background. Are you sure you were married at twenty?' Avril picked at her egg mayonnaise. She had decided not to become over tiresome as far as food was concerned.

'From my grand-daughter. She bought me an auto-biography of a past star. I wasn't really interested in reading it, but I didn't want to disappoint Paula. She rather disapproves of the books I read and possibly felt I had become addicted to them. I probably am: anyway, I read the autobiography and it has come in useful.'

'Yes, they are kinda trashy.' Avril referred to Lydia's novels. She had glanced through a couple of them.

'That's exactly what Paula says. Sometimes I read them twice. I put them down for a year and then go back to them. I know exactly what is going to happen but it seems to make no difference.'

'Do ya ever read the classics?'

'No – do you?'

'My husbands, or at least two of them, did, so I just helped myself to the main trend of some of them without reading all of the book. They're no different from your books, ya know. They deal with marriage, cheating, copulation, life and death. It's just a question of presentation, I guess.'

After this rather desultory exchange, the women ate the meal, for the most part, in silence. Avril, over the past 2½ weeks, had begun to talk less. Lydia talked a little more. A crude psychologist might have suggested that a certain amount of transference had occurred between them.

'You've never read much. You've hardly ever worked – I mean outside the home – you know, Lydia, it's not as though you are potentially clever. You are clever. It beats me where you get it from.' Avril had finished off the last piece of watermelon and was dabbing at her chin to remove the trickle of juice that her spilled over her bottom lip.

'I suppose it was from the children,' said Lydia.

'Ah, it must have been just wonderful, bringing them up, watching them grow, schooling, dating and all.' Avril waited expectantly for some bucolic insight into the maternal bliss she had never known.

'I only liked them up until they were about six or seven. I loved them as babies. I breastfed both of them. It was the only time I ever defied my husband. He wanted me to put them on the bottle. It really upset him to see them fastened to my breasts. I always had to feed them in another room if he was at home.'

'He doesn't sound so nice.'

'Henry? Oh, I think he was as nice as he could have been, but just a little set in his ways.'

'I loathe predictability. That's why you're such fun,' said Avril.

Lydia did not know what Avril had meant by her last remark, but demonstrated the truth of the observation by promptly suggesting that they should take an evening stroll along the harbour. Avril agreed readily. As they were about to leave their table, Ahmed returned with an envelope. It was addressed to Lydia and had remained uncollected at the reception desk for five days. She had not expected any correspondence – the letter had been forwarded from London. It bore a foreign stamp.

'It's from somewhere abroad. I don't know anyone outside England.' Lydia placed the unopened envelope on the table for Avril to see.

'Japan, it's from Japan! Aren't you going to open it?'

'It is addressed to me.' Lydia tore back the flap of the envelope with care and deliberation. 'Oh, oh.' A photograph fell out. Lydia stared at it for quite a time, and huge tears trickled down her cheeks. Avril was at a loss to know what to do. She picked up the photograph from the table. It was a picture of Lydia standing near an enormous statue which depicted two nude lovers. A Japanese name was written on the back and inscribed most formally 'With compliments'. Lydia had not mentioned that she had known a Japanese man. The inscription on the photograph was hardly endearing.

'Don't cry, baby. Don't cry, sugar.' Avril patted Lydia's hand but felt that her comfort was obsolete. Nevertheless, it seemed to help. Lydia dabbed her eyes with a table napkin.

'Shall we take the walk along the harbour?' Lydia got up from her seat.

'Sure, honey, sure. I'm ready.' Lydia began to leave. Avril touched her shoulder. 'Aren't you going to take this?' She held up the photograph.

'No, dear, you keep it – if you'd like to. I don't need it.' Lydia seemed to be decisive, and Avril placed the picture in her handbag. Either Lydia wished to forget the connotations the picture conjured up or she did not need a photograph to remind her. Avril took her arm and they stepped out into the night together.

They paused at a rail track. A huge steam-engine belched and snorted past, hauling what seemed to be endless numbers of freight trucks towards the port. It was ten minutes or more before they could cross the track. Progress was slow here. Once one had accepted that fact, waiting could be enjoyable. It was all a question of acceptance. Like brightly coloured butterflies glimpsing the world before entering chrysalis or death, they flitted together, hopping across the tracks, hovering but not settling. When they reached the high concrete wall, the huge gates which barred entrance to the two large ships docked to receive the freight were impregnable. They followed the curve of the harbour wall and expressed surprise when they reached the end of it. A smaller harbour stood sheltered beyond the wall. Tiny boats rocked at quayside moorings. Our butterflies had discovered a field of clover.

Fourteen or more small craft were moored at the harbour. Without exception all of them were old, and a studied glance showed up sections of rotted wood on the bows or hull. Endless woodwork patches dotted the hulks, and none of the vessels could comfortably have claimed to be seaworthy. It appeared that two or three men were allocated to each boat. At the most, there might have been four, and in the latter case the fourth member was always a pubescent boy. The fishermen were territorial, in that they were either on their boats or sat along the quayside space between it and the next one. A smell of cooking pervaded the air. If one man was cooking something on deck, the other held a hand line as he sat in the bows of the boat or on the particular patch of quayside that the boat snuggled into. Either they could not afford leisure or they gleaned enormous job-satisfaction from what they did. It seemed a strange thing to do in what time they had to spare. They did not talk a great deal but would occasionally call out one or two words to their partners. This greeting was met with a similarly sparse response.

The two women stopped at one such boat. They stood motionless, respectful of the silence. Avril was fascinated to watch the man on the boat. The glow from the primus stove lit up his features as he gently stirred the pot which hung over the stove. Steam drifted from its contents, and Avril found the aroma intriguing. From time to time he would look up from his cooking and meet her gaze. He would smile and nod and then return to the laconic preparation of his meal.

Lydia was more intent on watching the man who sat on the quayside. He held the hand line loosely between his thumb and fore-finger. The line was slack and he had not been ambitious. It entered the harbour water not more than four or five yards from the wall. He did not retrieve the line and cast it elsewhere. He sat and waited. Not once did he glance at Lydia. They returned nods. She was confident that she would bring him luck. She wished fiercely for something to take hold of the line. She hoped that Avril would not get impatient and want to fidget or move. A tightening of the man's lips and a tenseness which seemed to seize his body assured her that something was about to happen. She watched the hand line slip through his thumb and fore-finger, slowly at first and then it gathered momentum. He let the line slip through his fingers as it was propelled across the water. She saw the line tauten, noted the tug as a section of it sprang from the water. He began to wind it in quickly. His large, calloused hands moved deftly without fuss or complication.

'He's caught something. I knew he would,' said Lydia triumphantly. He must have understood her jubilation. He continued to wind in his line but grinned with pleasure at the way Lydia had expressed her delight at his good fortune. She smiled back at him.

'What do you suppose it is?' Avril could not detect any silvery fish scales, and whatever the man had caught had almost been hauled to the surface. Lydia saw the head appear from the water.

'It's an eel, a marvellous eel!' she cried.

Avril stepped back in horror as the black, wriggling, snake-like creature dangled in the air before their eyes. Lydia experienced no such trepidation. She seized on old sheet of newspaper which lay on the ground before her feet. As the man swung the eel onto the shore she grasped it within the folds of the paper. 'They're impossible to handle unless you do it like this,' Lydia called over her shoulder to Avril, who had retreated from the action. Lydia held the creature firmly. The man trusted her and wound up the rest of his line until he has reached where Lydia stood. He took the creature's head and snapped it back. There was a cracking sound, and the intense wriggling was suddenly reduced to no more than a quiver. Lydia handed him his catch. He held up the eel with one hand and extended his other one to Lydia. They shook hands, both delighted with the experience.

'My God, Lydia, where in hell were you reared? How d'ya know about that kind of thing? I feel scared just looking at the thing, let alone grabbing hold of it like that. Are they edible?' Avril's trepidation had been overcome by curiosity, and she peered at the joint prize the fisherman held.

'Oh, yes, dear, they're a delicacy. We eat them in London. When you visit me, I'll prepare some for you.'

Avril responded enthusiastically, not on account of the eel but for the invitation. Lydia had not mentioned that they might meet again, and Avril had been dreading the prospect of not seeing her friend again. Lydia's sojourn in Sousse was now limited to three days, and Avril knew she would be bereft after her friend's departure. The prospect of future times spent together dispelled this buried gloom. She enthused over the prospect of eating eels in London.

'And will we play darts, too?' she asked.

'Darts?'

'Don't you all play darts?'

'Oh, no dear, I've never thrown a dart in my life.' Lydia sounded surprised at Avril's question.

The man on the boat called out; the man on the shore answered him. He increased the cultural confusion of the two women by saying something to them in Arabic. The man on the boat gesticulated to the two women and pointed to his cooking-pot.

'I think we have an invite to dinner,' said Avril.

'They do eat rather late. It's almost midnight,' said Lydia.

'I guess they fish by night time. They do in Mexico.' Avril sniffed the air. 'Smells good,' she added.

'I think we should accept the invitation, although I'm not hungry. It's all so pretty and natural. We don't have to eat a lot.'

'I'm game, sugar,' said Avril as she watched the man pull in the boat towards the quayside. 'Just stretch your arms out, Lydia, and leave the rest of it to them.'

Avril had already been hauled into the boat's stern. The gap between the quayside and the boat, although not more than a yard or so, caused Lydia to feel hesitant. She had watched Avril fly across the space like the sparrow she resembled. Lydia looked at the black water that lapped the harbour's edge. The fisherman held out his hands appealingly. Lydia remained hesitant. The bovine nature of her frame warned her that they would have to be strong arms, indeed, to transfer her across the space of water successfully. She felt the man's hands grip her wrists as she edged forward and stretched out her arms.

'Jump now, Lydia!' Avril shouted encouragement. Lydia closed her eyes and obeyed. Her hesitant leap of faith proved successful. She did not even have recourse to stumbling as both her feet planted themselves firmly on the deck.

'Ya see,' said Avril. 'There's nothing to it.'

'Oh, I wouldn't say that, dear.' Lydia smiled her gratitude at the hands that had guided her safely through the air.

The light from an oil lamp lit up the proceedings which followed, and they were simple to the extreme. The meal consisted of a large mound of something that was half way between semolina and rice. It was flavoured with herbs and odd bits of fish. Avril had declared that it was called 'couscous'. Lydia found it rather tasteless in spite of the strong smell it exuded. Not that the eating of it was very difficult. One just took a handful and then ate at leisure. Two small handfuls were enough to satisfy Lydia's curiosity, and she was able to make her second helping last long enough to make it appear that she was not being impolite in refusing more of the food. The two fishermen ate heartily, and what scant remains of couscous were left over in the pan were quickly slung overboard. Some of the other boats had begun to start their engines, and the first of them had already left its moorings. A pool of light thrust from its bows as it left the small harbour's entrance.

'I think it's time our friends began work. It's the night shift.' Avril sucked some of the grains of food off her fingers.

Goodbyes were necessary, and the two women pointed to the shore and improvised hotel and sleep, using their hands, eyes and head as though they were a pair of untrained deaf and dumb adults. The fishermen understood them but returned a mime.

'They want to take us fishing! My God!' said Avril.

'I don't see what is so terrible about that, dear,' said Lydia.

'Lydia, when I say "Oh, my God", it doesn't always mean that I am appealing to Him. It all depends on the inflection I give it; otherwise it would be blasphemous.'

Avril didn't want to be cast as a damp squib on any pending adventure.

'What about tomorrow?' Avril yawned.

'Yes, I like something to look forward to: tomorrow will be better. We can bring them some small gifts. It's the custom if you accept hospitality.'

'Same in Japan.' Avril hoped that this remark had not reminded Lydia of the photograph.

The fishermen understood '*demain*'. The time for departure was stated, and the Atlantic was left in abeyance until the early hours of the following day.

On the way back to the hotel Avril noted how thin and scraggy the cats were.

'Cats, dear?' Lydia was feeling rather tired. She had never been too fond of cats or dogs. In this respect, she could have been considered not typically English.

'Forget it.' Avril knew there was no point in pursuing a conversation when Lydia was dreaming or whatever she was doing when she chose to be quiet.

Their late return to the hotel caused no consternation.

17

In order to be able to eat a little more couscous later on, Avril and Lydia chose to miss their evening meal. They had informed Ahmed at lunchtime. Initially he had displayed some upset, but when Avril unrolled their evening plans to him, he let it be known to them that their decision not to eat beforehand was a wise one. He also said that he had never been on a fishing boat himself, and from the expression on his face Lydia assumed that he did not find the idea exciting or even tasteful. She changed the subject of conversation, hoping Ahmed would forget their pending trip as his dining customers pursued their demands. Her hopes were not justified.

'George Mumbry says there is no insurance coverage for travelling on fishing boats. Apparently he thinks we're unfair to place such a worry on the tour operators. He says they wouldn't sanction the trip if they knew about it.'

Avril lay on her bed, eye-pads keeping her eye-lids closed. Both women had slept long into the late afternoon. Avril had awakened first and had decided to give her eyes a treat. Her mouth had rested long enough.

'George who?' Lydia asked drowsily from the other bed. She was still only half awake and found conversation difficult. Normally she always had to have a cup of tea before she could regain consciousness.

'Oh, yer know, Lydia, the Englishman, remember? We talked to them yesterday – or, to put it straight, you talked to them yesterday.'

'Yes, I remember him,' Lydia answered faintly, thinking of the reddening arms and the face that would peel like wallpaper. 'I don't see that it's any of his business what we do. We haven't told him that he could die from sunstroke. I think he is ignorant,' said Lydia.

'Oh, baby, that's a bit hard. I guess he was just a bit concerned about our welfare. He probably didn't want us to come to a quick end.' Avril laughed and had to readjust her eye-pads.

'A quick end might not be that bad. Most of us live beyond the age of being useful.' Lydia yawned and stretched her arms. 'Anyway, dear, we're well prepared,' Lydia added.

'What d'ya say?' Avril was frightened. She sat up and blinked the eye-pads from her face. If Lydia was referring to death, she should see a priest before they left the harbour.

'Well, we've got some nice presents. The clothes here are difficult to come by. I'm sure both men will be pleased with the shirts and pullovers.' Lydia roused herself into a sitting position and saw the traces of worry diminish from Avril's visage.

'Ya don't think anything will happen to us, then – do ya, Lydia?'

'Something will happen, dear. It's bound to on an adventure, isn't it?' Lydia answered her own question.

'Oh, no dear, I'm sure not. Think of the hundreds of times they have been out to sea. There's more risk getting knocked down on the road, or catching a nasty germ somewhere, than going on a boat trip. I'm sure it will do us both good.'

Lydia's total assurance as to their safety lifted Avril's spirits immediately. She was prepared to accept anything but the likelihood of death. This was odd, as her religion had taught her to think otherwise. In this sense, Lydia was much more of a Catholic than her friend. She accepted not only every day but every moment. Lydia did not find the idea of death shocking. Her own death was no exception. She kept these thoughts from Avril, who had thrust herself under the shower and had begun to sing.

'We're gonna be kinda late back. I mean very late.' Avril spoke, half apologetically, to the young woman at the reception desk. Lydia admired the woman. Her working day seemed endless yet she was always polite. Curt, perhaps, but always polite. The woman smiled at the gaudy elderly ladies as they paused at her desk.

'That is quite all right, madam. There are two night porters on duty. Enjoy your trip.'

'She knows about it, too. She doesn't look like an irres-
ponsible girl to me.' Avril had taken Lydia's arm as they
descended the steps of the hotel.

'I should think all the hotel knows, dear,' said Lydia.

'We should care, we should care. Ya know, I think it's
easier to be free at sixty than it is at eighteen.'

'Yes, you're probably right. It's a pity, isn't it?' Lydia
loved the evenings and looked up at the sky. Avril could
not answer her question.

18

Lydia felt a little concerned. They had reached the beginning of the waterfront of the tiny harbour. The tiny boats were dotted along the quayside as on the previous night. It occurred to her that the boats were not in the same position as the previous evening. She could not distinguish one boat from another. They all had so much in common. They were old. What paint they had ever received left a trace of colour here and there. It was like returning to a batch of patchwork quilts and seeking the original choice amongst diversities which made them all alike. Her bewilderment and confusion increased when she realized that she would not be able to recognize the fishermen. The faces had been lined, brown and weatherbeaten, but then so were all the faces along the harbour.

'Lydia, is my hair all right?'

As she spoke, Avril bent her arms across her chest, stuck out her elbows and made circular movements. Lydia watched Avril's shoulders revolve as though she were some featherless or oil-stricken seabird attempting flight.

'I wouldn't be worried about your hair, dear. We're not going to a dinner and dance.' Avril's question surprised Lydia. It seemed a silly thing to ask at such a time. Avril continued the bird movements as they strolled along.

'What a God damn idiot thing to do.' Avril scratched at her armpits.

'If you've changed your mind, dear, we can go back without any loss of face. I think we should find the two kind men first, though; then we can give them their presents and say one of us has a stomach upset.' Lydia felt dismayed. She had been looking forward to the sea.

'Changed my mind! Changed my mind! Do you think I'd want to chicken out on an evening like this? My God, whenever will I get the chance to do such a thing again? It's just that I've got mixed up with my sprays.' This last bit of information did not shed any enlightenment on Lydia's brain, which was now whirring with triple puzzlement. She was forced to be blunt.

'I'm sorry, dear, I don't understand you.' There was a slight edge to Lydia's voice. She had tried to keep it out. She did not wish to sound vexacious or to commence a quarrel.

'I have three sprays. One for my hair – just a gentle lacquer – one for my armpits, the other for . . . Well, I like to keep that part of me clean. Oh, don't get over-worried, I'm OK between the legs, but I've squirted hair lacquer under my armpits and it's kinda sealed my movements. I just wondered if I had frosted my hair with deodorant.'

Lydia touched Avril's hair and managed to inform her friend that it was free from anything before breaking into peals of laughter. Avril found Lydia's uncontrollable mirth infectious (she could laugh at herself), and the two of them found it difficult to walk, such was the extent of their hysteria. Their laughter acted like radar equipment. One of their hosts had heard and spotted them. By the time he reached them, their mirth had subsided but they were still a little breathless. He smiled in a formal way and touched his heart in greeting them. This strange movement caused both women to collect and organize their feelings accordingly. They shook hands and followed him towards his craft.

Newspapers covered the small section of the deck where the evening meal was ready and waiting. Two faded cushions had been borrowed from somewhere, and the two men gleefully produced two cardboard plates. Sensitive to the preparations that had gone towards their comfort, both women expressed their gratitude in quietly spoken English. The men understood the meaning from inflection and the quiet, almost sanctified delivery of the tone in which the two women spoke. The food was much tastier than before. The women ate more.

'This is good, real good. I don't know what fish is in it. I've tasted most fish but this is succulent, and just the one bone, no finicky bits to get in the way. It's real good. I'd love to find out what it's called.'

Avril flung a bone over her shoulder into the water, emulating the pattern set by her hosts. Lydia decided that she would tell her she had eaten an eel at some future date. No point in devastating Avril's imagination or chancing spoiling her appetite.

A bucket of water was produced for the women to wash their hands; Avril took the opportunity to douse her armpits. The fishermen accepted this action as though it were a religious ritual of some kind. They did similar things to themselves so that her odd action aroused no curiosity in them. The cushions were wrapped very carefully in newspaper. The excess newspaper and even the cardboard plates were not discarded. They were collected and stored in the hatch together with the meagre cooking utensils. Poverty created this sense of order, this sense of true valuation, yet meanness of any kind was absent. Lydia could not help thinking of her daughter and daughter-in-law. Try as she did, she could place no value on either of them. She had experienced some guilt over these feelings during the past months but now, as she helped fold the newspapers, her guilt vanished from her forever and her feelings only consolidated. One of the fishermen had started the boat's engine.

'We're going out. We're going out. We're going out to sea!' Lydia cried.

'And we're the first to leave, sugar. We're first off!' Avril replied as though their premature departure indicated some kind of advantage.

'We should give them their presents.' Lydia touched the neatly tied brown paper parcel which she had carefully hidden beneath the bows of the boat. The eyes of the fishermen had watched her place it there. She thought her action might have caused some curiosity. The fishermen had made no such display, as they had been busy preparing the meal, yet Lydia felt that her action had been noted.

'I guess we'd better open it. They can't be bothered with trappings, now.' Avril observed correctly that the fishermen were preoccupied with steering of the boat. The harbour outlet to the open sea was small, all but bottle-necked, and Lydia got the impression that the southern development of the town, the hotels, the tourists, the foreigners, people like that, had almost but not quite crushed the life out of the tiny fishing port. The small harbour and the fleet that remained resembled the post-script at the end of a letter, a reminder that had almost been forgotten or left out.

Both women wished to demonstrate their usefulness. Avril picked at the knots of string on the parcel and released the bonds without cutting any of the string. Lydia wound the string into a neat ball and folded the paper carefully. On behalf of their hosts, they practised an elegant economy. The paper and the string were stored safely in the hold.

A call from one of the fishermen indicated that they were past the harbour bottle-neck and into the open sea. The boat's rudder was tied in position. The course was set. The men were free to wait for a while. The sea was extraordinarily calm, and it was difficult to detect any sway on board. The moonlight gave more than adequate vision – indeed, Lydia thought that Avril looked luminous in her pale yellow shift.

'Are you going to give them to them, Lydia?' Avril held out the two pullovers and two shirts.

'I think I could give one set to the man at the rudder, and you could give the other to the man arranging the nets. Do you think that would make it more even?'

'Sure, honey, sure.' Avril took half of the offering and approached the man whose fingers were busy picking at the nets. He paused as Avril stood before him. She tapped his shoulder and for some odd reason half bowed. The garments were presented formally. The man held the shirt to him. He eyed the pullover. His pleasure caused him consternation. Apart from grinning, there was no way he could express his appreciation. He patted his chest, pointed to his own head. 'Habeeb, Habeeb,' he called out.

'Avril, Avril,' she called back. This demonstration was all but echoed from the stern of the boat. 'Naji, Naji,' answered by 'Lydia, Lydia.' The men continued shouting out the names of their passengers as the boat chugged outwards. Lydia Poulton of London and Avril Macey of San Francisco accepted this most romantic and original of accolades without the slightest trace of embarrassment. Indeed, many of their counterparts in their own native cities might well have considered them brazen.

The silence left both women in a state of awe. The boat's engine had been cut off. The lights of the town could be seen winking some ten miles from the shore. The boat was being allowed to drift. Work was about to commence. Lydia's nature did not allow her to be an easy onlooker, but watching Habeeb's first action she could think of no way of helping. If she or Avril had attempted to follow Habeeb's actions, they would have certainly hurled themselves into the sea. This would have been uncomfortable as well as time-wasting. The fishermen worked quickly, to an ordered haste. Occasionally they called to each other as they flung out a net which curled in the air and spread to its maximum before landing on the surface of the water. Each time the nets were drawn in, the silvery fish were despatched into the hold with breathtaking rapidity. When one patch of water had been scoured, the boat was allowed to drift to another region where fresh supplies might hopefully be found.

'We should use these, dear, and not just sit idly by while the men are working. I'm quite sure that every single fish counts. If we caught ten fish each they would be worth something. It would be a bit like one of the women in the book I am reading who is actually working her passage around the world on a Panamanian cargo boat.'

Lydia had begun to unwind one of the hand lines she had found whilst she was storing the string and paper. She passed one of the lines to Avril, who held it and looked at it with a degree of scepticism.

'Er – Lydia, the woman you were referring to, the one in your novel. She didn't work her passage in the cargo boat fishing, did she?'

'No, dear, she didn't.'

'I guessed not.'

Avril began to unwind her line, not because she had any faith in the reality of Lydia's suggestion but because she found the idea of it so typical of her friend, such a mixture of naïveté and practicality. It was impossible to block or blunt Lydia's approach to most matters. Observant to the last, one of the fishermen detected the action and placed a bucket containing some foul-smelling debris between the two women. He smiled his appreciation and returned to his nets.

'My God, what the hell is in that?' Avril held her head over the side of the boat where the air was fresh. The stench from the bucket was strong and rotting.

'It's our bait, dear. We just place some on the hook, then let the line trail. It's just the same as catching mackerel. There is little that you have to do. The fish hook themselves. Then you wind the line in. You'll know when you have a fish. The line will tug.' Lydia had already pierced a chunk of rotten fish on her hook. She cast her line into the water. Avril looked into the bucket and felt repelled.

'Look, baby, I don't think I can touch that stuff, let alone put a piece of it on the hook. I'm sorry.'

'There you are, dear.' Lydia did it for her, cast the line in the water and left Avril holding the wooden winder.

After twenty minutes or more, Avril had withdrawn her previous conclusions with regard to Lydia's naïveté and innocence. She was forced to overcome her revulsion and trepidation by the number of tugs her line received. The bait barely sank before it was necessary to wind in, unhook the fish, replace a little bait and repeat the operation.

'My God, you'd think these creatures never fed in their lives before.' Avril knocked the head of her twentieth fish on the side of the boat before removing the hook from its jaw. She had now become matter-of-fact about the procedure, and it made no more demands on her sensitivity than if she had been packing sardines in a canning factory. Avril realized this and was grateful for the more varied routine she had now come to accept. Lydia was pleased to see that between the two of them they had half-filled the basket with fish. By the end of the evening's fishing, their contribution would be small but nonetheless valid.

'I'll just catch three more. They will top up the basket.'

Everyone else had finished their labouring but Lydia seemed as obsessive about her fishing as some women of her age were about bingo or fruit-machines. 'There, that's the last. The bait has all but been used up, so we've left little

to waste.' Lydia unhooked the last catch of the early morning and let it flip into the basket. The men had drawn in
their nets and were preparing some kind of beverage. Avril
was content to rest and gloat with pride over her share in
the industry which lay in the basket near their feet. Lydia
took the basket in her arms and showed it to the men. The
shouted encouragement and satisfaction before Lydia
tipped the glittering contents into the hold.

'Ya know, the pair of us could easily go native.' Avril
spoke as she and Lydia washed their hands in sea water.
She sniffed at both her hands. First one, then the other, and
her nose wrinkled. 'They still smell kinda fishy but I guess
I'm almost used to it. It's not so bad once you're familiar
with it.' She dried her hands on the bottom of her shift. This
action she copied from Lydia.

The men joined them, sitting close, cross-legged. They
held a mug in either hand. Habeeb passed one of the mugs
to Avril, and Naji passed one to Lydia. Even at this social
level the fishermen had kept to a demarcation. Lydia
observed from this that they wished now to be considered
separately. Naji had sat opposite Lydia, and she could not
help but be aware that he had let the toes of his right foot
touch the edge of her shift which spread about her as she
leaned back on her haunches.

'This stuff's so strong you could use if for stepping up a
flat car-battery.' Avril was referring to the coffee, which
was over-sweetened yet bitter to taste. At each sip,
granules were left behind on her tongue. She sipped more
in order to be rid of them; the wash down only replaced the
ones that disappeared down her gullet by another layer.
She smiled politely. If only Habeeb would take his eyes off
her, she could have a damned good spit and tip a little of the
coffee overboard. Lydia felt the toes curling and uncurling
around the bottom of her shift. Habeeb's feet were playing
a similar orchestration on Avril's garment. Coupling had
commenced.

Somehow they managed to consume the coffee. Avril
was relieved to place the mug down. The bottom of it was
full of sediment, and Avril really felt as though she had
been drinking from an urn that was attached to the

seashore. She licked her teeth in order to be free of the irritating grains. Other boats chugged past them, and both women watched the decrepit fleet crawl its way towards the harbour. Now there were no lights from other boats that they could see. Their boat still drifted, the engine dormant. The men sat quietly and stared. Avril swallowed hard.

'Lydia, what are ya thinking?'

'Probably the same as you, dear.' Lydia looked at Avril's face as she spoke. In the early morning light it appeared waif-like and vulnerable. There was a sweetness to the expression that Lydia had not seen before. No wonder she had had four husbands. She was appealing, so small, so . . .

'Lydia, are ya scared? I mean, just a bit scared?'

'No, dear, I'm not. Are you?'

'I guess I would be if I were on my own, but we're in this together. I don't think that they want to harm us, but . . .'

'Yes, I think you're right. They wouldn't hurt us but they're waiting for a . . . a . . . They're waiting for a gesture from us. That is what they are waiting for.'

'Yeah, I know. How d'ya feel about it?' Avril could feel the pressure of Habeeb's knee rubbing against her thigh.

Two gulls screeched and squawked, wheeling overhead. Lydia looked up at them. Predatory birds. She spoke as one swooped horribly near them.

'I'm going to tell Naji that I would like to see the engine of the boat before we return. I'm not at all apprehensive about what will happen down there. I know what will happen. I'm going to accept it as part of the trip. It's not something that could easily happen off the coast of Britain. If the idea upsets you, I won't do it. In a way I couldn't, because I'm sure that if Naji shows me the engine, Habeeb will want to show it to you. Are you shocked, dear?'

'Hell, no. If you're going to see the engine, I'll inspect the stern. I don't want to be a follow-up job. Better if it's simultaneous, don't ya think?'

'Yes, dear. I really don't think it will take very long. It seems silly to keep them in suspense any longer.' Lydia hauled herself up and pulled Naji on the shoulder. She pointed to the hole leading to the engine-room. He followed her. Even before she had both feet in the dark recess, he was clutching at her flesh, squeezing her bottom and pumping her breasts with his hands. The position was far from comfortable. Her shift had been lifted. Her knickers were off. She felt him thrust himself twice inside her, felt his frame twitch, heard him mutter something in Arabic as he groaned, and knew that it was over.

It took more time getting out of the engine hatch than it had to get through what had occurred inside it. It took all of Naji's strength to heave Lydia's buttocks with his shoulder in order to lever her successfully back onto the deck. She crawled out on all fours. Avril was standing near the entrance and watched her friend emerge. She helped her to her feet. The engine of the boat coughed twice and then began to chug. The men began to sing.

'We're getting a serenade thrown in, too. You name it, Mrs Poulton, and we've done it.' Avril spoke almost triumphantly.

'I don't think it's a good idea to put names or labels on things – that is, unless they're for sale in shops. If you want to call this evening and its events by a name, where would you begin, dear? It will never happen again and . . .' Lydia stopped. 'It's almost light and I'm not a bit tired. When I was a young girl . . .'

Again Lydia stopped talking. The gulls had distracted her. She listened to the voices of the fishermen. The sounds were almost as harsh as the noise from the birds. Avril took her hand. She surmised, correctly, that her friend was dreaming again. Like children they remained with their hands together until they were safely deposited on the quayside.

'Our shifts are ruined, Lydia. Just look at the state of us.' Avril gazed at herself in the large mirror of the bedroom at their hotel. Lydia took stock of the patches of oil that had left indelible stains all about her own dress.

'Oh, Lydia, there's fingermarks all over your behind. It looks as though someone has done a hand-printing exercise on you!' Avril pulled her shift over her head and let it fall in a heap on the floor. Lydia had to struggle more with hers, but finally freed herself of it. The two pieces of coloured cloth lay in crumpled heaps side by side.

'I guess we're not gonna use them anymore,' Avril remarked sadly.

'No, dear, they've served their purpose. Pity to waste the cloth, though. They would make nice kites.'

'Ya what?'

'Kites for flying, dear. You know, the children use them.'

'Yeah, yeah, I know, honey.' Avril could not always keep track of the startling flights of imagery that Lydia's imagination directed conversation towards. One minute you were bemoaning the loss of a dress and the next minute you were flying kites.

Smelling of fish, spotted with oil and dust, they both scrubbed and washed under the shower. Avril was talking but Lydia could not hear her above the splashing of the water. Neither of the women was aware of the other's nakedness, and neither of them realized that this, too, was a new experience. The steam rose and their bodies occasionally touched.

'Ya know, Lydia . . . I think that man . . . most men . . .'

'Yes, Avril?'

'I think that most men are a bit . . . a bit . . . er . . . er mmm . . .'

'Pathetic?'

'Ya. That's it. Pass the soap, would you?'

19

Nancy had been a courier for nine years. She had taken on the job after a short-lived marriage with a partner who was earning a great deal of money from his employment in a large advertising agency. Her husband had always exuded confidence, wit and charm. He had been entertaining between bouts of exhaustion and depression, clever with the use of his earnings and rather neglectful in his role as a husband. He had been unfaithful after they were married. Nancy had thought she could be broad-minded about such matters, that she could accept his 'little bits on the side' as part and parcel of his work. Therefore, it came as a great shock to her when she needed to visit the doctor for tranquillizers. She could not sleep when her husband stayed out all night. Eventually she was reduced to only two options: divorce or mental hospital. She chose divorce – her husband found the proceedings less traumatic than she did. He even smiled and shook hands afterwards. Nancy had wept.

Eventually she had worked out a recovery programme based on lining all her emotions with asbestos. Her job as a courier helped her. She was never still and managed to relate to customers without expending any of the resources that her husband had drained from her. Consequently she was never shocked or surprised whatever the situation she was confronted with. There was always a procedure for everything. Nancy actually enjoyed wearing her uniform. It placed her in permanent disguise, total hiding.

She had forgotten what Mrs L. Poulton looked like and was more than a little puzzled when the driver leapt from the bus to greet the guest who was departing from the Grand Hotel du Sud. Normally he was an idle bugger and would not leave his seat to help with the luggage. It was odd. Particularly as Mrs L. Poulton represented her last pick-up. There was no one else staying at the hotel who was due for return to London. They used the building only for cancellations or quick bookings, and this did not occur often. Nancy looked out from her vantage point on the coach, a single seat near the driver.

A lot of the hotel staff were grouped around the entrance way, including several waiters, a couple of uniformed porters, a girl receptionist and a thin, tall Tunisian wearing a beautifully cut light-weight, expensive Parisian suit and dark glasses. Nancy recognized him as the hotel manager. The time was a strange one for a manager to appear, unless there was a guest from the Tunisian Tourist Board arriving. (Such officials were always welcomed and treated like foreign royalty.) Eleven in the morning was not a usual time for a manager to impress his presence.

Nancy sighed. She hoped the ceremony would not take long. She dabbed her brow with a cologne pad. It was always essential to look cool. It was the hat that caused her to perspire, but the thought of removing it while she was on duty represented anarchy. Nancy would have none of that. She looked with idle curiosity through the open coach door and explained to the sweating passengers that they would not have to wait long.

'Mrs Pooolton.' She heard the driver call the name as a plump, bronzed-looking, middle-aged lady came out of the entrance. She was accompanied by a small, scraggy lady of quite indeterminate years. The hotel staff were busy shaking her hand and, without any doubt, were making the most effusive farewell Nancy had ever witnessed. The manager presented her with flowers. Mrs Poulton was followed down the steps by all the company. What on earth was the woman doing dressed like that? Nancy's eyes widened as the scarlet shift, silver necklace and golden, turned-up sandals came startlingly into view. Only a crank or an aristocrat would dare enter London in such a state. Tunisian hotel proprietors did not take kindly to cranks. The woman must be important. Nancy stirred herself. If there was some special importance attached to the woman, a certain prestige, a fame, she ought to know of it. She left the bus and held both hands out in greeting as she met Lydia on the pavement.

'Hello, dear.' Lydia greeted Nancy by giving her a flower from the bunch she had received from the manager. She selected the bloom with care. It was then that Nancy remembered her. The woman could have been anybody's mother. She hadn't even bothered to drop her off. In fact, she had almost forgotten to collect her. She was the only 'P' on the list.

'Good morning, Mrs Poulton. I hope you have enjoyed your stay.' Nancy reverted to jargon and format. For some reason Lydia caused her disquiet. It was impossible to fathom out why, except that to all intents and purposes Lydia's change was so dramatic that Nancy felt cheated by the impression that the older woman had previously chosen to convey.

'I'm Avril Macey, Mrs Poulton's – er – Mrs Poulton's sister,' the scraggy woman in the lemon shift introduced herself. What was she doing with an American accent? Nancy's puzzlement increased.

'I'm sure it's against the rules, and believe me, honey, I'm not one for breaking rules, but I wonder if you would mind if I accompanied her to the airport?' Avril had already followed Lydia, who had boarded the coach. Lydia settled herself on the same seat next to the driver and made room for Avril to perch herself on the corner by squeezing close up to the window.

'The plane departure is from Monastir.' Nancy did not want to state that extraneous passengers were not allowed. The driver took his place and smiled at the women sitting close to him.

'Yes, dear, we know,' said Lydia.

'Don't worry, honey, I'll get a taxi back. Sure, I know you won't worry about little old me. There's not enough of me to take up anyone's seat.' Before Nancy could negate Avril's suggestions, the driver had revved his engine and the bus had begun to move. Lydia waved to the hotel staff, and Nancy returned to her seat near the door. She dropped the flower that Lydia had given her and bumped her head on the handrail as she bent down to retrieve it.

'Are you all right, dear?' Lydia had seen Nancy's forehead crack against the metal bar.

'Yes, yes, I'm fine, thank you, Mrs Poulton. I'm fine,' Nancy answered quickly but untruthfully. She was shocked and surprised. Why did the bloody woman pretend to be so ordinary? Nancy felt as though one of her passengers were a spy and looked forward to the time when she could deposit her at Monastir. She knew that some holiday visitors could be unpredictable, but this one . . .

'Lydia, I'm frightened.' Avril looked directly into the great windscreen as she spoke. The road was free of traffic and the bus bore them swiftly along. The vehicle was in perfect condition. There was no chance of its breaking down. Avril had given up all such hopes. Nothing could detain Lydia now. Lydia placed her flowers at her feet and put her arm about Avril.

'Frightened, dear? What are you frightened of?' Lydia sensed that Avril's fear was real.

'Of being alone. It was different before. I've never had any problem relating to people and I've always kept myself busy. But now . . .' Avril placed her hand to her mouth in case her words might deteriorate into a sob. She removed the hand. The sob never came. Bird-like, she turned her head quickly to look into Lydia's face. 'Damn it, Lydia, I've gotten used to ya. Don't ya understand?'

'Yes, I do, dear. It's been such a lovely holiday. It wouldn't have been anywhere near as nice without you. Don't worry, we'll meet up again.' Lydia spoke soothingly but without condescension.

'When?' The airport had come into view. Avril could not keep the panic from her question.

'Didn't you say you were coming to London after Rhodes?'

'Yeah. I'm spending one week in the city of Rhodes and one week in a place called Lindos. Both places are full of history, just like me.' Avril could not posture enthusiasm for holidaying alone. 'I wonder if I can fly direct to London from Rhodes?'

The bus turned into the airport's coach bay. Avril fiddled nervously with the sleeve of her shift.

'Of course you can, dear. Why, you'll be in London

within four hours of getting on the aeroplane. Really, you're so close, distance is nothing when you're flying. You have your breakfast on Rhodes and your lunch with me in London. I'll wait in all day. It will be a Tuesday when you arrive.' Lydia gathered her flowers from the floor. Already some of the blooms had begun to droop. She sighed. 'I came in with flowers – I mean, I was given flowers when I entered the country. People have always given me potted plants in England. I know they last longer.'

'What?' Avril's anxiety had lessened with the certitude of Lydia and London. She had even been given the day. Nothing to worry about now. 'Ya what, Lydia?' Avril repeated her question.

'Potted plants, dear. They last longer than cut flowers but I prefer cut flowers. Now I suppose I have to join my group.'

Lydia was aware that the coach had emptied. Nancy had marshalled her entourage into a squad and was fixedly smiling at Lydia. The driver, loyal to the last, had placed Lydia's case well in the forefront of the group. He helped both women off the bus and saw Lydia to her case. Nancy beckoned and the group trailed after the woman in the Napoleonic hat. It was time for Avril to retreat.

'I'll see you Tuesday fortnight, dear,' was all Lydia said.

Avril watched the scarlet shift move slowly out of sight through the customs enclosure. It had paused at the customs desk. The flowers seemed to get in the way of the procedure. Nancy had cause to intercede in some discussion before Lydia finally passed through.

'Oh, Lydia, Lydia Poulton. What a gal you are!' Avril smiled and muttered before turning away to hail a taxi.

'She must have missed the aeroplane. She's not among the group. I never felt that easy about this idea in the first place.' Eileen's voice rose in accusation. Barbara, Derek, Eric and Paula stood beside her and scanned the returning Dalmar Tour Group. Lydia could not be seen among them.

'There's no need to get in a state . . .' Barbara was not allowed a lecture.

'I'm not in a state,' Eileen snapped, demonstrating that she was.

'We must contact the tour operator and send a cable. Even that may not be necessary. Mother might have been diverted onto another flight. There could be any number of explanations. In all probability, it will be just some simple hitch in the travelling arrangements.

'She might be ill. It would be awful to be ill in Africa.' Eileen was still intent on some dramatic or tragic circumstance being proved that would make Barbara squirm. As it was, her sister-in-law didn't look her usual self-confident self.

'I'll check with the tour operator,' said Derek.

Paula lit a cigarette. 'There's no need to do that.' She inhaled so deeply that she began to cough.

Derek made to carry out his own suggestion. Paula restrained him, holding on to his arm, unable to speak for coughing and giggling.

'Paula!' Barbara hissed.

'Gran is there. I can see her. It is her. I know it is!' Paula pointed to the lady in the scarlet shift standing slightly apart from the tour group. The lady stood quite still, quite passive, like some immigrant who was waiting for her legality to be approved. 'That foreign-looking lady is Gran. It looks as though she's changed her style. Shall I wave to her?' Paula enjoyed watching the horror seep into the faces of the four adults.

'Well, if someone will collect her, I'll sort out the car,' said Eric. Barbara made no attempt to hinder his quick exit. Derek followed him.

'They've left it to us. Oh, what does she look like!' Eileen gibbered on as her discomfiture increased.

'This just confirms my original opinion, Eileen. Mother's mind can't be right. I can't bear to look at her.' Barbara had no option. Lydia had noticed Paula's wave and waved back. Lydia advanced towards her kith and kin.

'I've had such a lovely holiday. I can't tell you how nice it all was. So comfortable and . . .'

'Mother, it's raining outside. Did you have some other clothes?' You could change in the toilet.' Barbara cut Lydia short, and Eileen looked at Lydia's scarlet attire, jewellery and pointed sandals with unveiled disapproval.

'What happened to your hair?' was all Eileen could contribute.

'I had my hair cut.' Lydia flicked open her suitcase. There seemed to be very few clothes in it. Barbara was sure that her mother had left London dressed in a blouse and skirt. There was a raincoat, too. Lydia fished out a plastic mac.

'There's no point in my going to the toilet, dear. I gave most of my clothes away.' Lydia put on the plastic mac, adding further incongruity to her appearance.

'Gave them away?' Eileen croaked.

'You've no idea how poor people are over there, my dear. They buy mostly secondhand clothes, and even they are expensive. Just a few dresses, skirts and a blouse or two. I didn't take many clothes with me. I wish I had. I've really far more than I need.' Lydia clicked the catches on the suitcase shut as if to say there was no more to be said on the matter.

'We had better hurry, Mother. We don't want to get caught up in the afternoon rush hour. It's this way.' Barbara strode quickly forward. Eileen caught up with her and strode forth at her side. Lydia trailed a few yards behind her relatives. Her case was not heavy but she correctly surmised that the two ladies who were escorting her home would rather not appear related to her or, indeed, appear to be accompanying her. Lydia, some time in the past, might have felt uncomfortable about the embarrassment she was now causing. Paula took her grandmother's arm.

'There's no need to rush, Gran. I know where the car's parked. Bugger those two.' She nodded in the direction of her mother and her aunt who had almost quickened their pace to the extent of a trot.

Lydia paused at a book kiosk. 'Oh, good, dear. I'd like to get a book. I left the others with my friend.'

'Your friend?'

'Yes, dear. I have a friend in North Africa.' Paula gulped at this information and shook her head slowly as her grandmother purchased a book with a lurid cover. In deference to Lydia's years the kiosk assistant placed the book inside a paper bag.

'I bought this for you, dear. It might be as well if you unclasped it now.' Lydia touched the heavy silver necklace which hung about her throat. Paula unleashed the heavy clasp and held the necklace in her hands. It was heavy, raw but quite stunning in its beauty.

'It's beautiful. It's the most beautiful . . .'

'My friend said you would like it. Come along, dear, it's selfish of me to keep the others waiting. You'd better not mention the necklace to your mother. I didn't buy presents for anyone else. Not that I didn't think of it, but there was nothing suitable, nothing quite right for them.'

Lydia was 'dropped off' at her home like a sack of hot potatoes. She let herself in. Her relatives were behind with imperative domestic schedules. (No, they wouldn't come in for a cup of tea.)

Barbara was irritated with her daughter, who for some unaccountable reason had begun to cry. It was not like Paula. Probably calf-love. Adolescents were so unaware of the shallowness of their feelings and were all too inclined to inflict them on someone else. Barbara did not question her daughter's tears. In the meantime, Paula fingered the necklace in her pocket, smiled and continued to weep.

20

They must be dead by now. Lydia was thinking of her flowers as she sat in her kitchen. She had placed them too carefully beneath the underside of the seat in front of her. Aeroplanes did not provide easy storage for flowers. It was terrible to think of them dying there without any water, no one to enjoy them. Perhaps one of the cleaners would take a fancy to them. Lydia had not changed into European clothes and found it necessary to light the gas fire. She shivered a little as she struck the match. She crouched near the amber glow and warmed her hands, enjoying the sensation, and the gentle hissing of the flames seemed to have a mesmeric effect upon her. It was difficult to say how long she remained like this.

'I suppose the temperature change is a bit of a shock, Mrs Poulton.' Lydia had not heard Stephen enter the room. In all truth, she had forgotten he was staying in her house. She blinked.

'Is anything the matter?' he asked.

'Oh no, dear, I was just getting warm. I must have been dreaming. I mean, I must have looked awake and dreaming.' Lydia stood to greet him.

'You look, you look different.' Stephen avoided saying that Lydia looked younger. Somehow he felt this would have been tantamount to an insult.

Lydia looked down at her feet. 'I suppose I do, but I don't think that much different from before I went. At least, I don't feel that much different. It sounds silly, but I think I've got to know myself better while I've been away on holiday.'

'You mean, you know what you want from life?'

'Oh no, dear, no.' Lydia sat down and ran her fingers through her cropped hair. 'Life, life. I don't know what I want from it. In fact, I know little about it. Barbara has said as much to me on many occasions. Knowing what I wanted would mean planning ahead – I mean, a long way ahead. I've never done that, dear. It's not too good an idea as far as I'm concerned, as I change course with events. And I'm not responsible for the events happening most of the time. This last part of my life is just proving more eventful,' Lydia pulled her chair closer to the fire, removed her gold sandals and began to warm her bare feet.

'You're not bothered about your destiny, Mrs Poulton?'

'Call me Lydia, dear. No, I don't think I am, but then I don't think I understand you, Stephen. I've never been clever.'

Stephen did not pursue these abstractions any further. He plugged in the electric kettle and began to arrange the table for a meal. Five plastic containers were placed down the centre of the table, the same amount of space left between each one. Stephen put out the plates, brown bread, cutlery, a butter dish and a currant cake.

'I've got tea ready. I thought you might be hungry.' He peeled a layer off the container nearest to him. 'I'm sorry, I'm no cook. I bought all these from the delicatessen shop. The lady behind the counter said they would make a nice tea. There's a different kind of salad in each box.'

Lydia was hungry. She joined him at the table. 'This is very kind of you, Stephen. There's far too much for the two of us.' Lydia thought of Eileen's scant offerings and added, 'Better too much than too little. If there's any over, we can always put it in the fridge. Pass the bread, dear, and I'll cut it. How many slices?'

'Two, please.' Stephen had uncovered the remaining containers and begun spooning the different contents onto their plates.

'It all looks so pretty,' said Lydia, looking at the assorted mounds on her plate. Stephen poured out the tea and they ate.

Lydia had expected him to ask about her holiday and was quite ready to extol the joys of North Africa to him. She was more surprised than disappointed that Stephen chose not to mention or ask after her holiday. He behaved as though she had not been away at all. This meant that most of the meal was spent in silence. Some people might have found this uncomfortable, just the sounds of the slurping of tea and the odd noises that the mastication of food made. No wonder people talked at meal times. Lydia chewed on bovine, unembarrassed by the absence of conversation.

'It's nearly five. Do you mind if I leave you, to watch the football results?' Stephen had already risen from the table. Lydia did not mind. She called after him.

'Of course not, dear. I know how you feel. I was just the same about watching horses, myself; not now, though. Strange how you can lose interest in something. I suppose it has to do with . . .' Stephen had left the room and Lydia saw no point in talking to herself. She helped herself to a second cup of tea and another chunk of cake. She found herself looking at Stephen's empty chair and thinking of Avril Macey.

It was past 10 p.m. Lydia had unpacked what few belongings she had brought back with her, washed her underwear and taken a long bath. She discarded her African attire for a warm European housecoat and put on some scent. No one could say that Lydia was addicted to anything but she did enjoy the late-night horror film on Saturday television. She settled herself in the lounge, turned on the set but left the sound untuned. She would wait for the film to start before letting any noise impede her from reading the book she had purchased earlier in the day. She had digested two chapters and was not sure whether or not she had read it before. Her usual concentration on her reading-material strayed, and from time to time she looked up at the newsreader on the television set. As there was no sound, she watched him mouthing the words. If I become very old, I may go deaf or blind . . . Lydia introduced herself to a first lesson in lip-reading. She found it astonishingly difficult. She stared more intently on the moving lips. How quietly people's lips moved. The task she had set herself began to take on hypnotic proportions. The tap on the lounge door startled her.

'Come in,' she called out, and quickly opened her book.

'I made some cocoa. I thought you might like a cup.' Stephen had spilled some of the drink into the saucer.

Lydia took the cocoa from him and emptied the saucer's content into her cup.

'Thank you, dear.'

'Sorry, I managed to spill a bit of it.' Stephen stood awkwardly, and Lydia wondered what he wanted to say. Whatever it was, he couldn't say it. Lydia swallowed some cocoa and tried to help him.

'Oh, the late film is starting.' She pointed to a lion that roared silently from the screen. 'Would you like to watch it? You're very welcome, dear.'

Stephen coughed and shuffled his weight from one foot to another. 'No, no, thanks. Thanks all the same, no. Goodnight, Mrs Poulton.' He left the room, barely giving Lydia time to bid him goodnight. Lydia climbed from her seat and turned up the volume – perhaps Stephen was still upset about Paula. The man obviously wanted to talk about something.

A coffin had flown out of the back of a black coach drawn by four horses. The driver, in his frenzy to make the horses move faster, had not noticed he had lost his luggage. The film had commenced and Lydia drowned in comfort and fantasy.

The last wooden stake was driven through the vampire's body and the film ended with a suitably blood-curdling scream. Lydia had been rather disappointed. It was as well that it had ended in a scream or she might have dozed off. She turned off the set and yawned. She felt more fatigued than usual. The film had been more of an opiate than a stimulus. On the other hand she had gone through an exhausting day. She brushed her hair and put a little cream on her face before getting into bed. Normally she read a little before turning off the bedside light. She sighed heavily and abandoned her usual routine, clicked off the light and closed her eyes.

Lydia knew she was dreaming. She had dreamt it all before but a long time ago. She must have been a child when it first came to her. It was a simple dream but a horrid one. Its recurrence had made it worse. Also, the struggle to awaken herself from it had always left her exhausted. The dream had gone from her in her late teens and, now, here it was again. She was falling, falling from some sickening height. She knew that her body would not hit the ground yet sought to break the fearful sensation by breaking into consciousness. It seemed to take her a long time. At last she was free of it. The fingers of her right hand were gripping the side of her bed. Her head had slipped from the pillow and hung awry near her right hand. She was breathing heavily. The dark room comforted her. She adjusted her pillow and lay on her back. What a relief. It might have been the after-effects of the flight that had brought it on. Her breathing steadied and reverted to normal.

It was at this point that Lydia realized that someone else was breathing as heavily as she had been. Someone was located somewhere in her bedroom. No, how silly, how very silly, thought Lydia. Nevertheless, she held her own breath and studied the expected silence. There was breathing; there was breathing in her room. She waited no longer. She pressed her bedside light switch and flooded the room with light.

'It's me, Mrs Poulton.'

'Yes, dear, I can see that.' Lydia sat up in bed and viewed Stephen, who stood near the open bedroom door.

'I never heard you knock. You'll catch cold standing there like that.'

Lydia looked at Stephen. He wore only his Y-front underpants and some black socks. Lydia smiled. He reminded her a bit of Charlie Chaplin, not by his attire, nor his physical appearance – indeed, Stephen was a tall, bony man. It was his pathetic stance which brought the late comedian to her mind. Stephen frowned.

'Don't laugh at me, please. Please don't laugh at me, Mrs Poulton.' He spoke quietly.

'I'm sorry, Stephen. It was just that you reminded me of someone. I'm glad you're here. Did I call out? I expect I must have done. I was having a bad dream, a nightmare. I haven't dreamed for years. If I have, I have no recollection of them. I was falling.'

'Falling?'

'Yes. In my dream I was falling, down and down. I suppose I must have cried out.' Lydia sat up in bed.

'No, you didn't,' said Stephen.

'I didn't?' Lydia placed her hand to her throat and looked more intently at Stephen. He had crossed his arms about his waist. His thin frame shuddered.

'Here, place this coverlet around you.' Lydia took hold of the bedcover and began to tug it from the top of the bed. Stephen helped complete the operation. He still remained standing and draped the coverlet around his shoulders.

'You look Arabic now, much more Arabic than a lot of the Arabs I saw.'

Lydia's attempts at being jocular were frozen by Stephen's lack of response. He clutched the garment closer about him and sat himself on the bottom corner of her bed. He began to pick at his nose. Lydia ought to have been revolted but both her children (when they were very young) had done this. 'Are you pulling the pictures down?' she used to say. Stephen was not only pulling the pictures down but examining them on his nail before flicking them on the carpet. He was as preoccupied with this process as only a three-year-old child could have been. Lydia gently interrupted the nasal warfare.

'Is anything the matter, dear? Is there anything I can do to help?'

'Will you look after me? Just for a few days. Yes, that's what I want. I want you to look after me. For a time. I'm sorry.'

Stephen let his head hang forward as though he were attempting to bury his eyes in his chest. Lydia responded immediately.

'Of course I will, dear. Now, don't you worry any more about it. Everybody needs looking after at some stage. I don't mind in the least. I have . . .' Lydia stopped talking as Stephen cast the coverlet from his shoulders on to the ground. He walked round to the side of the bed. Lydia watched him pull off his socks. He discarded them quickly, nervously, and she could not help but look at the black, woollen balls that now lay on the carpet. Stephen pulled back the sheets of the bed. To her own surprise Lydia made no remonstration. She merely moved over a little to make space for him as he lay by her side. He switched off the bedside light.

'You're very warm,' he whispered. 'You smell so good. I've always liked the way you smell.' He settled himself against her, his hard frame pressing and sinking into the acres of soft flesh. He buried his head between the huge breasts, thrust his face and head into the cleavage. Then his mouth sought her left nipple. She suckled him, held his head to her. The fact that he had removed his underpants was irrelevant. For the rest of the night he slept free of anxieties, and Lydia was not troubled with any more nightmares.

21

Lydia paused in the hallway. The shopping bags had caused both arms to ache. The effort of carrying them had left her a little out of breath. She placed both bags on the hall floor and glanced at her wristwatch. It was four in the afternoon. This gave her two hours more to herself before Stephen arrived home. Deduct one hour for preparing his meal and she was left with an hour. Time enough for a little read. How precious an hour could be. She counted on her fingers – nine days. He had said he wanted looking after for a time, but not for how long a time. As for the evenings, the night time – well, they held no excitement. His affection (if it could be called that) was something private to him. There was no question of his wishing a response from her. She had received more satisfaction from her babies seeking her breasts than she had from him. An adult baby was less satisfying than a real one.

When Lydia entered the kitchen, she immediately dropped one of the shopping bags. A can of baked beans and a few potatoes rolled across the floor. Stephen retrieved them and placed them back in the over-turned bag before setting it aright. Lydia had not expected to find him home. She put the other bag carefully against the wall. She was able to hide the flush of colour that had risen to her brow and cheeks. Of course, he could not have read her thoughts in the hallway. This did not prevent her blushing.

'Home early, dear?' Lydia saw that his two suitcases were standing beneath the kitchen table. She looked at them and then at him.

'Yes. I'm leaving, Mrs Poulton,' he said.

'Aren't you going to stay for your dinner? It won't take me more than an hour.'

'No, I'm not hungry.'

Lydia was surprised at his response. His appetite previous to this moment had gathered in momentum daily. He had even put on a little weight. Lydia sat down. She sensed that he wished to give an explanation quickly and get out fast. The expression on his face resembled that of some of the people who were waiting for buses. Buses that seemed intent on not arriving. Lydia felt like a 106 bus – she had arrived and could travel.

'I saw Paula today. She had been waiting outside the lecture room for me. She wants us to be together again. I don't know that I can ever forgive her, but I've agreed to it on a trial basis. I told her I was staying at your other house. She is calling round there at six. You don't mind her staying there, do you? Of course, we'd naturally pay you a little more rent. I owe you some money for food as it is.'

'Oh, forget that, dear. I'm not short,' said Lydia, feeling relieved and cheated at the same time.

'You're not upset, are you?'

'Upset? No, it was what I had expected.' Lydia had not known what to expect but thought that, given the circumstances, this was the safest answer she could proffer. Stephen sighed, pulled his suitcases from under the table and took up one in either hand.

'I'll be off, then.' He struggled past her and stood for a moment near the kitchen door. 'Oh, er, er, you won't mention anything to Paula about, er, er, er, m . . .'

'No, Stephen, I won't.' Lydia's decisive tone reassured him.

'Cheerio, then.' On reaching the outside door he called back.

'I forgot to tell you. A telegram arrived for you. It's on the kitchen table.'

Lydia cupped her chin in her hand and rested her elbow on the table. The telegram? She opened the packet quickly.

COMING TO LONDON A WEEK EARLY NO POINT
IN BEING ANYWHERE WITHOUT YOU
ARRIVING AROUND FIVE PM
                       AVRIL MACEY

There was an address on the telegram. It was a hotel in Lindos. Lydia felt suddenly elated. She must answer immediately. She took out some notepaper and began her letter there and then, sitting at the kitchen table.

'My dear Avril, Dearest Avril, Avril my dear' – try as she would, Lydia could not commence the letter without opening it as though it were a love letter. How absurd. How ridiculous. Lydia was about to begin when she heard the front-door bell ring. She knew who it was. Her arithmetic had always been poor. She screwed the notepaper up into a tight ball and thrust it into her coat pocket. She made a conscious effort to keep calm as she walked the length of the hallway. Her heart pounded. She opened the door.

'Sugar honey, I've missed ya so!' Avril Macey's face was streaked with tears. The two women embraced. They kissed on the doorstep.

'Come in, dear, come in. I'll carry the bags. You must be worn out. It's lovely to have you here. I'll make us a cup of tea. I haven't enjoyed being alone, either.'

'I guess we'll stick together for a time,' said Avril.

'Oh, I'm sure we will,' said Lydia, as she closed the front door.